REDEEMING JUSTICE

PETER O'MAHONEY

When you live so close to the edge, you have to be prepared to fall over it.

Redeeming Justice
Bill Harvey Book 1

Peter O'Mahoney

Copyright © 2024
Published by Roam Free Publishing.
peteromahoney.com

ALSO BY PETER O'MAHONEY

In the Bill Harvey Series:

FIRE AND JUSTICE
WILL OF JUSTICE
A TIME FOR JUSTICE
TRUTH AND JUSTICE

In the Joe Hennessy Legal Thriller Series:

THE SOUTHERN LAWYER
THE SOUTHERN CRIMINAL
THE SOUTHERN KILLER
THE SOUTHERN TRIAL

In the Jack Valentine Series:

GATES OF POWER
THE HOSTAGE
THE SHOOTER
THE THIEF
THE WITNESS

In the Tex Hunter Legal Thriller series:

POWER AND JUSTICE
FAITH AND JUSTICE
CORRUPT JUSTICE
DEADLY JUSTICE
SAVING JUSTICE
NATURAL JUSTICE
FREEDOM AND JUSTICE
LOSING JUSTICE
FAILING JUSTICE
FINAL JUSTICE

REDEEMING JUSTICE

BILL HARVEY
LEGAL THRILLER
BOOK ONE

PETER O'MAHONEY

CHAPTER 1

The black sedan stopped one block shy of its destination, the narrow streets packed with patrol cars, the flashing lights blinding eyes. Ten patrol cars, at least.

Bill Harvey jolted out of his car, slammed the door behind him, and ran through the warm September air. Despite the warmth, despite the heat from the Californian sun, Harvey didn't ditch his coat. It was his safety blanket, and in that moment, he needed all the comfort he could get.

Closer. He reached the yellow tape around the perimeter, stepping under the tape with confidence, but a fresh-faced police officer held out his hands to stop him.

"Detective Pitt wants me here," Harvey stated firmly.

The officer stared at him and then nodded at his colleague to check with the lead detective at the scene. The officer was quick to return and let him through.

Closer now. The tears were forming in his eyes, the sweat gathering under his thick coat, and the nervousness was growing in his stomach. With this many officers, it felt more like a terrorist attack than a crime scene.

"Harvey." One of the officers grabbed his arm. It was Detective Ramos. They had never liked each other. "I'm sorry."

Without acknowledging Ramos, Harvey continued to the living room.

"Harvey. Wait." Detective Matthew Pitt stepped forward to stop him going any further. "That's as far as you can go. We're still processing this crime scene and can't let you in there."

"Tell me you have a lead."

"We have a lead."

"Who?"

"Harvey." Pitt placed his hand on Harvey's shoulder, directing him away from the living room of the regally styled house. "Mary is in the kitchen. She needs you to comfort her. She needs to be taken away from here, and she asked for you. She wanted you to be one of the first to know. And I think she liked the idea of having a lawyer here. You can make her feel safe."

"Is she a suspect?"

"Mary? No, of course not. She has an alibi, and I couldn't imagine her doing something like that. You should go to her."

"I need information first."

"Of course, your mind is always working." Pitt rubbed his brow and looked away. The LAPD Forensic Science Division members pushed past them, ready to analyze the frantic crime scene. "He was a good man. He had the respect of everyone in the department. Not many judges have been as well-liked as he was."

"Tell me what happened, Pitt." Harvey's voice was still firm.

Pitt drew a long breath, stepped closer to Harvey, and kept his voice low amongst the activity. "I know he was your mentor. I know that you and Hardgrave were very close. We—"

"Tell me what happened," Harvey repeated.

"Earlier today, Hardgrave was shot in his living room at close range. One bullet between the eyes. Mary found his body lying in his new orange armchair—just delivered this morning. Blood is all over it. Killed instantly. He wouldn't have felt any pain, Harvey."

"Time of death?"

"It looks like he's been dead for eight to ten hours."

"Cameras?"

"They've all been switched off. The shooter knew what they were doing."

"Witnesses?"

"None."

Wailing came from the kitchen. It was the desperate cry of a woman who had lost her companion, friend, and husband.

"Harvey." Pitt reached across and grabbed his arm. "There's something you should know."

"Go on." Harvey's words were cold, as were his emotions.

"I saw you talking to Carlos López this afternoon. He has connections here. We have a lead, and it points in his direction."

"López? How?"

"Hardgrave's estranged daughter, Michelle Hardgrave, is the girlfriend of Juan Lewis. That's where we're looking. Lewis, of course, is closely connected to Carlos López and Roberto Miles. All three of them have been seen together on many occasions. And rumor around the department is that Hardgrave tipped off the police this morning which led to your client's apartment being raided. This is off the record, but Lewis was supposed to be in there today with a briefcase full of drugs. Except Lewis wasn't in the apartment... so your client has to take the fall for the drugs."

"Not López. He walked away from the game a long time ago. He did his time and came out a changed man. López has spent the last nine years working in drug rehab centers. He's not a killer. He's out of that game."

"Maybe. Maybe not." Pitt shrugged. "But he's connected here somehow. Lewis, Miles, and López were all big players once. These are dangerous men, Harvey. Very dangerous. Be careful."

"I can look after myself."

"Of course you can. Just tread carefully. Lewis and Miles are still two of the heavy players on the East L.A. drug scene. I don't think you know what you're getting yourself into. These people are well-connected, and those connections run very high up."

"Are you saying that this murder was drug-related?"

"No." Pitt stopped talking as another detective walked past. Once the hall was clear, he began again. "But judges don't just get shot. This isn't a robbery, and it isn't even close to being an accident. This is a targeted hit. Whatever Judge Hardgrave was involved in—"

"He wasn't involved in anything."

"Of course." Pitt looked at the ground. "Mary is shaken up, Harvey. She needs someone to take her away from here. She asked for you."

"You'd better chase down this killer quickly." Harvey's words were cold again. "Because if you don't, I will."

CHAPTER 2

The tone of L.A. traffic was more frantic than usual.

On the drive to his office, Bill Harvey was verbally abused twice on the roads—once by a fervently swearing mother with two young children in the back of her car and the second time by an old lady who couldn't see where she was going. He had never heard such foul language come from a woman with pink rollers in her hair.

Neither incident was Harvey's fault, but his drive included middle fingers, horns, and enough swear words to make the Pope faint. Not that it was anything unusual for L.A. traffic.

"Hello, Kate. Any news?" Harvey stepped into his office, greeting his secretary.

The office was spacious and well-lit, and with Kate's artistic design touch, it felt contemporary. With two large abstract pieces of art on the walls, the room was inspiring for staff and impressive for clients. The spacious office in Downtown Los Angeles reminded him how far he had come.

From the days when he first came to the city, working as a hypnotherapist in what was formerly known as South Central L.A., to now owning his piece of this great city. It was an office that crime and justice had paid for, at least in one way or another.

"No news yet, I'm afraid," Kate smirked. "Have you got anything to report?"

"Only that you look amazing today."

Kate Spencer brushed a loose strand of blonde hair behind her ear. Despite her natural beauty and her easy smile, compliments hadn't always come her way. Her now ex-husband did everything he could to drag her confidence down. After being called ugly on a weekly basis by the man she once loved, her self-esteem was shattered, and it had taken a long time to rebuild her love for herself. Looking in the bathroom mirror was still a painful process.

"I'll have you know that I'm a lot more than just my looks,' she said sternly. "I should be judged on my talents, not just my appearance. I'm a very useful employee, and I would like to think that I'm here for more than being just a pretty face." Her stern eyes looked up to her boss. "I should be respected for my work, not my looks."

"I know you're an intelligent, smart, feisty, and witty woman who is very capable of doing this job… but you also look mighty fine today."

Even when he had to deal with society's lowest level of scum—the murderers, thieves, and psychos of L.A.—Kate's genuine smile lightened his day.

And without her skills, he would be a disorganized mess.

"Thanks, boss. You too." Her shoulders shrugged a little as she accepted the compliment. "How was the funeral for Judge Hardgrave?"

"Horrible." Harvey slumped into the chair opposite his secretary's desk, usually reserved for clients. Despite working in this office for the past four years, it was the first time he had sat in the chair.

"You didn't stay for the wake?"

"I hate those things. I hate the idea of being forced to talk to so many grieving people that I've never met before. There are hugs, and tears, and way too many emotions. I would much rather be here working."

"Emotions aren't your strong point," Kate mumbled. "Have they arrested anyone for the murder yet?"

"Not yet," he responded quietly, gazing at the floor.

Reflecting on the loss of his mentor, associate, and friend, Harvey stared into nothingness. After he'd graduated as a lawyer, Judge Andrew Hardgrave was the first judge Harvey stood before. In his first case, Harvey had been a nervous, fumbling mess—the opposite of what he was today.

Hardgrave had seen some of himself in the young lawyer and offered to mentor him in the legal process. That relationship had grown into a genuine bond between two strong males, and their monthly dinners became the centerpiece of stability in their busy lives.

The funeral hit Harvey hard. The smell, the air of discomfort, and the constant sobbing almost broke through the strong wall around his heart. His distant father had helped him build that wall. 'Caring for something will make you weak, boy,' his father had repeated at the dinner table over and over. His father's funeral was a low point in his life, and he'd hated funerals ever since.

But Harvey was reaching a time in life where he was attending more funerals than weddings, seeing more sad tears than happy ones. This was the fourth funeral he'd attended that year, with not one wedding to balance it out. He would much rather be watching two people enter into a legal agreement to make each other unhappy for the rest of their lives than listen to the painful cries of a devastated widow.

Nothing was as soul-destroying as listening to a widow cry.

"They must have a lead, mustn't they? They must have something?"

"Not even close. They're scared. The cops are scared. The detectives are scared. The whole department is afraid of these guys. The leads they have related to this shooting are very well-connected people, and the detectives know that they have to step lightly in this case, or they'll be shot themselves."

"But that's their job."

"They're still just people doing a job. They have families they want to go home to at the end of the day. They've got their own children to protect. I don't blame them for stepping lightly." Harvey had the greatest respect for what the men and women in blue did for their city's safety, even if they hated him for defending the people they tried to lock away.

"Do you think the connections go all the way up?"

"Maybe, but personally, I think Hardgrave was the top of the tree."

"Are you saying that he was on the take? He was a dishonest judge?"

"Not a chance. He was too straight for that. I think he was being used, and when he was no longer of use, someone killed him."

Kate gazed at the man she had adored for so long. There was an aching, a vulnerability, in his eyes that she hadn't seen before. She wanted to hug him, to tell him everything would be alright, because she could see under that tough-guy exterior, he was hurting.

But she couldn't do that. Her boss wouldn't dare show any weakness in public.

"I'm sure they'll get the job done." Kate tried to soothe him. "The police won't let this case go cold. It's too big a case; it's in the paper every day. They can't let a judge's killer get away with it. They'll get him. I'm sure they will."

"I wouldn't be so confident." Harvey stood and began making his way to his inner office. He paused and looked back at his faithful supporter. "But we will help them find the killer. We'll do what they can't, go where they won't, and then we'll hand them the evidence to make an arrest."

"Where would we even begin?"

"At the start." His voice was firm. "And our first lead arrives in twenty minutes."

CHAPTER 3

Law books lined one wall, psychology books on the other. Between them sat the sum of that knowledge: a lawyer whose patience was wearing thin. Not that patience was his strength.

Harvey sat behind his large desk, tapping his foot impatiently, his eyes never leaving the door. The afternoon sunlight flooded through the window behind him, warming his back slightly, and the computer desktop next to him glowed annoyingly. He hated computers. Never trusted them. He would much rather have a desk full of files than one electronic document.

"Your five o'clock appointment is here," Kate buzzed through on Harvey's phone system. The moment had arrived.

"Send him through."

Carlos López was slow to move. He rubbed his shoulder, an old injury, before sluggishly making his way through the glass door that led into the office of his criminal defense attorney. Dressed in jeans and a shirt that had absorbed a lot of sweat over the years, he didn't even manage a smile to greet his defender.

He'd lived life hard, but he'd lived it well.

As a former hypnotherapist, Harvey had spent years reading people and their reactions, and he could see that Carlos was a man with a hard past. His face had more wrinkles than a typical forty-five-year-old, and he was almost devoid of any smile lines—the effect of a life lived in serious business.

"Carlos López. It's nice to see you again." Harvey greeted him at the door with a handshake.

"Hello, Bill. I've had a tough morning. I could really do with some good news today."

"I'm afraid I can't help you there, Carlos. Just more questions." Harvey walked around to the front of his desk, picked up a pen, and leaned against the wall, intently watching his client's reaction. "What do you know about Judge Andrew Hardgrave?"

Carlos López's face reacted with a look of confusion as he sat in a comfortable armchair. "The murdered judge?"

Harvey didn't offer a response.

"I never met him."

Harvey waited. Silence can be an amazing weapon in pressuring a person to answer.

"Look, I never met the judge directly, but I've known his daughter for a while," Carlos conceded. "I've heard his name thrown around a bit over the years. Judge Hardgrave's daughter, Michelle, has been dating my cousin for years. They have a really on off relationship, but I think they're back together again."

"Juan Lewis?"

"That's him. She's been dating Juan for a long time, but from what Juan told me, she wasn't close to her father. She hardly talked to him, although Juan liked to encourage them to chat. He liked being connected to high-powered people."

"Did Lewis ever mention Judge Hardgrave?"

"I don't know where you're going with this."

"Answer the question." Harvey was firm with his client. A man with a hardened past like Carlos López didn't react well to a soft touch.

"Like I said, I've heard his name mentioned a few times." Carlos waited for Harvey to respond, but he didn't. "Lewis would talk to Hardgrave, and Hardgrave would keep him updated on a few things that have been happening around the city. It was a give-and-take relationship between the two of them."

"Are you saying that Judge Hardgrave was dirty?"

"No. Not even close. Hardgrave would just answer a few questions for Lewis, like who would be the best cop to talk to about getting information. Or if any targeted investigations were going his way. Nothing serious, and nothing that could get Hardgrave into trouble. Just a helping hand here and there."

Harvey didn't appreciate his mentor's name being dragged through the mud, but for the sake of gathering information, he kept his emotions in check. "And what would Hardgrave get out of giving Lewis information?"

"Seeing his daughter, Michelle." Carlos rubbed his shoulder again, rolling his arm backward. "If Hardgrave helped Lewis, then Lewis would make sure that Michelle came to the meeting. From what Juan told me, the judge adored Michelle, but Michelle hated him. This was the only way he could see her. She would never just go by herself."

"That makes sense. Hardgrave had wanted nothing more than his daughter's forgiveness. He'd spent the last ten years of his life trying to redeem himself for all his past mistakes, and nothing had mattered more than his daughter. Her forgiveness never came." Harvey sat down behind his desk, his hands flat on the table. "Your name was mentioned in connection with Juan Lewis, and Lewis was mentioned in connection with the Hardgrave murder."

"Just because he's my cousin doesn't mean that I'm connected to everything in his life."

"But you're close with him?"

"He's family, yes. We speak on a weekly basis."

"And you would cover for him, if needed?"

Carlos didn't answer the question. Instead, he looked away, moving a pen holder slightly on Harvey's desk, dispersing his nervous energy. It was a sure sign that he wasn't giving an honest answer.

"Maybe." He coughed loudly, a deep ache caused by years of smoking more than a pack a day.

The honest answers had stopped, and Harvey realized he wouldn't get any more information out of the Mexican-born Californian just now. Slowly, he leaned back in his chair, staring at Carlos with a sense of authority.

Carlos avoided eye contact, squirming to find a comfortable position. When it was clear who was in charge of the room, Harvey turned his attention to the current file.

"Carlos, I'm going to be honest with you about your case, because that's how I prefer to work. I don't like to string a client along." He opened a folder in front of him. "I've reviewed the file on your drug possession charges, and things don't look good for you. The prosecution seems determined to send you to prison for this one."

"What? The drugs weren't mine. They weren't mine." The fear began to build in Carlos. Prison wasn't where he wanted to spend the next four years. "I had never seen that briefcase before. Never. It wasn't mine. How can I be charged for something I had nothing to do with?"

The terror of the orange jumpsuit was real.

"Carlos, I've contacted the right people and conducted the preliminary investigations. There isn't a lot for me to go on in this case. Now, I could sit here and sell you hope. I could sit here and fill you with confidence about the future—telling you all about the freedom that you'll enjoy—but I'm not going to do that. I'm not giving you a false hope about this case. Instead, I'm going to give you the truth. And the truth is that you're in trouble."

Carlos stared at Harvey intently—this meeting certainly wasn't going the way he'd expected. He had been through the system twice before, and it was not a journey he had enjoyed.

Ten years ago, he'd faced the legal system for the first time. He was nabbed on the street carrying a small amount of drugs and spent a year behind bars. That year changed him; he reformed. He found God, got clean, and transformed his life on the inside.

He was the perfect example of what prison could, and should, do.

But he ran into trouble with the law again four years later when he was arrested on a reckless driving charge. In desperate need of help, he'd typed 'Good lawyer in L.A.—cheap' into Google, and Bill Harvey's name was the first to appear. Harvey had a smaller office then, just him working out of a tight, dark, messy space in Downtown. He didn't even have Kate back in those days. But Harvey was a tireless worker, and the more cases he took on, the greater his reputation grew.

And the bigger his reputation grew, the bigger his

office had become.

He took Carlos' reckless driving case and proved that there was no willful or wanton disregard for safety on Carlos' behalf. He was merely driving fast because his mother had just been admitted to the hospital after a fall. Unfortunately for Carlos, he'd crashed the car on the way and made the rest of the journey in the back of an ambulance. At least he got to lie next to his mother as they worked on his broken leg.

"I'm innocent. Isn't that what you're supposed to do? Get innocent people off charges? Isn't that why we have a legal system?" Carlos leaned forward on the desk, desperate for his voice to be heard.

"Carlos, the police raided your apartment and found a briefcase full of heroin. That heroin has a street value of $50,000, and you haven't offered a valid explanation for how the drugs came to be in your apartment. That isn't a good start, but it gets worse from there."

"I've offered an explanation. They planted it! The police planted the drugs. How many times do I have to tell you that?"

"That's not good enough. That explanation isn't going to get you off these charges."

"They weren't mine! That should be the only explanation that you need."

"There's a lot of evidence in your drug charge case and not much explanation. That's not a good start. The police need probable cause to press charges, and in court, we need to eliminate any reasonable doubt, so that gives us a head start when the case goes to court. The problem is that no matter how large our head start is, we don't have much hope of winning this case. We need a lot of things to go right for us before we even consider taking this to court."

"Then why would I pay you? Your services aren't cheap, my friend."

"You pay me because I'll get you the best outcome for this case. That, I can tell you with confidence. However, the best outcome may be to do a deal with the prosecution. We have to consider that option. And that deal may still involve going to prison for a period of time."

"I can't do this." Carlos gripped his chair tightly. "I can't take on this stress."

"We'll do the best we can, Carlos. We'll—"

"I need a cigarette." Carlos abruptly stood and walked out the office door, fumbling for the smokes in his pocket. The pressure had hit him hard. Life as he knew it was about to be taken away again.

After Carlos had stormed past her desk, Kate popped her head into Harvey's office. "Is he coming back?"

"He'll be back in a moment. He's gone out for a smoke."

Kate gently shut the door. "Did you get anything from him? In relation to the Hardgrave case?"

"He didn't say anything directly, but I got the information I needed. The people he associates himself with are killers, cold-blooded killers. Any investigations into this case are going to push into risky territory. If we're going to do this, if we're going to find this killer, we need to be ready for that. This is going to get heavy, Kate."

"You wouldn't have it any other way."

CHAPTER 4

"To give ourselves the best chance of winning, I'm going to ask you to explain everything to me." Harvey leaned back in his chair, tapping his pen on the edge of the desk.

"Like what?"

Carlos stunk of smoke as he sat back down. He'd quit smoking a year ago, but the stress of this case had reawakened his need for nicotine. In the ten minutes he'd been standing outside the building, he'd smoked six cigarettes, one straight after the other.

It had done nothing to calm his nerves.

"I need to know everything about that night, and you cannot hold anything back from me. In the conversations between you and me, we're covered by attorney-client privilege. As you have been through the legal system before, I'm sure you're aware of it; however, I'll go over it again to make sure you understand. The privilege allows us to have full and frank discussions about the case without the threat of myself, the attorney, being compelled to testify against you. This honest transfer of information will enable me to give you candid advice and effective representation. However, the privilege doesn't cover us if the discussions are used to commit further crimes. Do you understand?"

"I understand."

"Good. Then, we'll start with the facts. Your apartment was raided on September 12, and the police found $50,000 worth of heroin inside a briefcase in your apartment. There were no residents present at the time of the raid, so it's assumed that the briefcase belonged to you. If the drugs weren't yours, can you tell me who they belonged to?"

"No." Carlos shook his head.

"Then, can you explain how the briefcase came to be in your apartment?"

"No, I don't have an explanation for that. But I'll tell you that it wasn't mine. I didn't put it there, and I had never seen that briefcase before in my life. It didn't belong to me, and I was surprised by the police raid and even more surprised when they arrested me."

"Who else had come into your apartment in the previous twenty-four hours?"

"Just myself and…" Carlos paused before he answered the next question.

"Who?" Harvey pressed.

"My cousin."

"Juan Lewis?"

"Yes. My cousin and I were the only people in that apartment within the previous twenty-four hours. That was nothing unusual. Lewis has been to my apartment many times over the years." Carlos coughed loudly again; the years of smoking his greatest regret.

Harvey paused, drumming his fingers on the table. "First things first—we need an explanation of how that briefcase came to be in your apartment."

Carlos' voice rose as he presented his argument: "The police put it there. The guys that raided the place. They put it there. They had to. There is no other explanation."

Harvey had heard that same statement many, many times before. It was normal for a defendant to claim that he was set up, as they had seen it a hundred times on television, but in reality, it was very rarely the case. He closed his eyes for a long moment and shook his head slowly.

"Even if that was true and the police planted those drugs, that won't help us in court. Nobody would believe it, and even if we had evidence to prove that this was the truth, the prosecution would never let us win. If that sort of case looked like it was going to get through, we would have every level of government in the United States working against us. Nope. Sorry, Carlos. That isn't a defense we can use."

"They did it, though. These guys are the real criminals. They planted it."

"Even if they did, we can't use it." He paused as a question ran through his mind. "But why would they do it to you? Why would they choose to set you up?"

"They were after Lewis."

"Go on."

"Juan and I used to be business associates. But I did my time for the crime. I committed a lot of crimes before I went to prison, but prison changed me. I've been out nine years now, and I've never committed another crime. I'm out of that game. I know a lot of people come out of prison worse off, but not me."

Harvey usually wouldn't believe a speech like that—he had heard that kind of talk before—but there were two things about Carlos that convinced Harvey he was telling the truth.

Firstly, Carlos' eyes spoke the truth.

Secondly, Carlos had spent the last nine years volunteering at the drug rehabilitation center in East L.A. His work there had been tireless, and he had done it all without a cent of pay. He had poured his life savings into supporting The East Rehabilitation Center and even had a room named in his honor. Harvey had visited the center as part of the previous case, and all the staff had raved about the work that Carlos did. He had changed lives for the better.

It was clear to Harvey that Carlos was a reformed man, working hard to make up for the mistakes of his past.

"I know you spend your time volunteering with drug addicts, trying to get them back on the right path—"

"I love it. It's my calling. It's what I was meant to do with my life. I've done a lot of evil in the past, but this is my redemption for all my past wrongs. I was meant to help these people out and make their lives better. When I was trafficking drugs, I caused a lot of pain to a lot of people. I didn't know that then, but I can see it now. Back then, it was all about the money to me. I wanted more of it. All of it. I couldn't get enough money, but that led to me getting caught and being sent to prison."

"You carry a lot of guilt for dealing drugs?"

"Absolutely. I watched a friend's son wither away from addiction just before I went to prison. That changed me. Watching someone's child die because of something you deliver is heart-wrenching. My decisions destroyed many, many lives. I might not have pulled the trigger, but I killed people. I'll never forgive myself for putting drugs on the street, but the best I can do is work hard so that other people don't have to watch their children go through the same thing."

"That's a touching story, Carlos. I might get you to talk about that story in more detail if we decide to put you on the stand. Would there be people at the rehabilitation center who would testify to your good character?"

"Of course. We're a family there."

In horribly messy handwriting, Harvey scribbled notes on his pad. He used to worry that the client might be able to see what he was writing, but he had since realized that it takes a non-trained eye many minutes to decipher what he had scribbled. "So you think the police were after Juan Lewis?"

"Lewis made the mistake of making the wrong people angry. He thinks he's invincible sometimes, but he annoyed some of his high-powered connections. So they wanted to grab him for a crime and put him away for a very long time. That's what the police were going for. They didn't want me; they wanted Lewis."

"What I don't understand, if that was the case, is why they would have planted the drugs in your apartment. Why not plant the drugs in Lewis' apartment?"

"Because his world is tightly controlled. He has hidden video cameras everywhere. They know that. If they tried to plant drugs at his home, he would have been able to prove that they did it. So they planted it at my apartment, which he owned, when they expected that he would be there. They thought we were in the apartment. That's why they did it."

"So you're saying that they raided your apartment on the notion that Lewis was present?" Harvey raised his pen in the air to make a point. "But he wasn't there. I doubt the police would make a mistake like that, especially if they were trying to set him up."

"We were supposed to be in there. They saw us enter the apartment, but they didn't see us leave. We left through the laundry room window and ended up in the parking lot next door." Carlos leaned forward to make his point. "You see. They thought we were in the apartment."

"Why would you leave via the laundry room window?"

Carlos hesitated. "Because."

"Why?"

"Because that's what we decided to do."

"Sounds very implausible."

"It's the truth."

Dropping his pen, Harvey didn't press any further. His client believed that the police had set him up but had no evidence to prove it. He may have convinced himself of the reasons for the raid, but a personal belief wasn't enough to win a case.

Whether the drugs belonged to Lewis, Carlos, or the cops wasn't Harvey's concern. His only concern was how he could do his job and how he could win the case.

He stood, turned to his large window, and looked at the streets below. He loved this view of his city. The streets were buzzing below, full of life and flavor. He loved feeling like he was in the middle of the action in the country's second-largest city.

"Tell me, Carlos, why keep your connections to Juan Lewis? He's known as a big-time dealer in your part of L.A. You're obviously passionate about drug rehabilitation, but your cousin is the one causing people to become addicted. If you know he's causing pain still, why keep that close bond?"

Carlos shrugged and looked at the wall. "Lewis and I are family. We've known each other our whole lives. We came across the border together as kids from Mexico, and everything we did, we did together. We're a team. Always have been. We're family, and although our lives have now taken different paths, we're still brothers at heart."

"Until you got caught."

"If Lewis could have gone to prison for me, he would have. You can't end a bond like that overnight. Lewis and I still talk most days of the week—and most days, I tell him to get out of the game. But he wouldn't know what to do with himself if he wasn't 'Juan Lewis—The Boss'. He's stuck in that life. And that's OK. I turn a blind eye to that for my family." Carlos took a moment to look around Harvey's spacious office. "Did you read all these books?"

"At one point or another, yes, I've read all these books. Some are law books; other ones are based on psychology. They're not light fiction."

"You like reading about psychology?"

"Human behavior fascinates me. I love watching a person react to hard questions. Body language tells me so much more than words."

Carlos squirmed at the uncomfortable notion. The first half of his life had been built on lies. It was a life of drug dealing and surviving. Truth only got in the way of his success.

"They weren't mine. That's the honest truth," Carlos stated again, trying to convince his lawyer of his truth. "How can I even be charged when the drugs weren't in my possession? They haven't proved that I had those drugs, have they? I wasn't carrying them at the time. Isn't that what you can say?"

Most criminals denied their guilt.

Even the ones who had been caught on camera denied their guilt until they realized there was no use fighting. Half of Harvey's job as a defense attorney was to get innocent clients off, and the other half of his job was to get the best deal for the ones that he had no chance of getting off.

Right now, he was positioning for the best deal.

"You're lucky they're only charging you with possession. With this amount of drugs, they could have charged you with the intent to distribute them; however, I imagine they don't have enough evidence to push that forward. They're taking you for possession because that's their strongest chance."

"I'm supposed to feel lucky?" Carlos grimaced. "I didn't even have the drugs on me. How can they charge me with possession when they weren't in my possession?"

"Drug charges can fall into many different groupings when they reach the court. Actual possession is what it sounds like—the actual possession of narcotics involving hard evidence, which is found by law enforcement officers on the person. In that sort of case, the question is less whether the defendant may be found innocent or guilty and more whether the officers had sufficient probable cause to justify conducting a search. The concept of constructive possession is less straightforward, and that's what we're looking at here. It doesn't involve the presence of tangible physical evidence on the person. Instead, constructive possession involves two key components that can be used to point to the possession of narcotics: the defendant must have knowledge of the drug's physical whereabouts, and the defendant must have the ability to exercise authority and control over the drugs in question. That's what they're saying with your case."

"That's stupid. The law is stupid."

"That's your opinion, and maybe the jury feels the same, but the prosecution is sure on this one. They found the briefcase in your apartment and are arguing you had knowledge of it being there and that you could exercise control over the drugs. They're going to bring you down unless we broker a deal with them."

Carlos wiped the thin layer of sweat from his brow with the back of his wrist. "What's the deal?"

"The police want you to testify that the case belonged to Lewis. They have made that very clear. Like you said, they're not after you. They were tracking Lewis that morning, and when they saw he entered your apartment, they raided the place. Our problem arises because they didn't see you or Lewis leave the apartment. You didn't walk out the front or back door. When they went through the front door of your apartment, they thought they'd pinned the case on your friend. And when they found out that neither you nor Lewis were there, and there was no further evidence that the case belonged to Lewis, they were left with no option but to charge you with the crime. But that gives rise to another question. Where did you go?"

"We went to the diner that we always frequent: El Mejor. We were there from ten in the morning until late in the afternoon. We drank coffee, ate tacos, and talked about life. That's what we did all day. Nothing unusual."

"Interesting." Harvey turned from the window and quickly scrawled more notes on his pad. "If you give up Lewis as the owner of the briefcase, then we can get you a very good deal. We might even be able to get you off completely. But you have to testify against your cousin and state that the briefcase belonged to him."

"Like I said, that's not going to happen. Lewis and I are tight. He's my family from Mexico. We would never do that to each other. I couldn't sleep at night if I did that to my family."

"That's the only deal on the table. They'll put the squeeze on you until you give up who the drugs belonged to. They're not after you, Carlos. They couldn't care less about you. All they want is the person who is dealing the heroin on the streets. They want to bring the whole house down. They want you to turn over on Lewis."

"You know I can't do that."

"And there's no chance you're going to plead guilty?"

"None. I'm innocent. The drugs weren't mine. I'm not going to prison for a crime I didn't commit." Carlos was firm. "I'm not pleading guilty. Never. I didn't do anything wrong. Your job is to get me off the charges. That's why I'm paying you the big bucks."

Harvey drew a large breath, filling his lungs with the cool, air-conditioned air. His job would be a lot easier if everyone just told the truth.

But then, if everyone just told the truth, he wouldn't have a job at all.

Watching Carlos closely, Harvey leaned on his hefty oak wood desk and let the silence sit in the room. The way a man reacted under the cloak of silence said a lot.

Carlos looked comfortable.

In fact, he seemed too comfortable. He was either very confident of his innocence, or he was overly confident in the judicial system.

Either was dangerous.

"We can take this to court, but I wouldn't recommend it. The odds are very much against us. Firstly, we need to explain to the court how $50,000 worth of drugs ended up in your apartment. Do you have any reasonable explanation that might convince a jury?"

"The postman dropped them off?"

"No." Harvey shook his head, in no mood for jokes. "Does anyone else share the apartment with you?"

"No."

"Any regular visitors?"

Carlos shook his head. "None that I would blame the crime on."

"We will have to fight for lack of intent or lack of knowledge for the possession. I could explain that you picked up the suitcase by accident. Have you done any recent travel by plane or bus?"

"I flew to New York last month."

"Too long ago. No jury will believe that you picked up a suitcase by mistake and then took a month to open it. No, that won't work. But how about a taxi ride?"

"Yeah, sure. I take taxi rides all the time."

"Right. That might be our best option. You picked up a briefcase out of the boot of a taxi, and clearly, you picked up the wrong one. How long before the arrest did you catch a cab?"

"I think it would have been the night before."

"Perfect. We will have to check the surveillance footage around your apartment building and make sure that the prosecution can't disprove our theory with the footage. Otherwise, we might have the smallest of chances."

"That's getting better. I knew you would be worth the money."

"Now, they'll bring up your connection to Juan Lewis in court. He's the man they're actually after, and as your alibi for the time of the raid, I have no doubt that they'll subpoena him and get him on the stand under oath."

"He'll say whatever he needs to say."

"I'm going to need to talk to him." Harvey's statement was firm. "The prosecution is going to subpoena your cousin to the stand as a witness, and we need to make sure that he's ready for their questions. They're going to go after him, and his responses are going to be very important for our case."

"I don't think that's a good idea." Carlos stared at Harvey for a while, waiting for a response. "But if you have to talk to him, be careful. My cousin has a mean temper; he snaps very quickly. Even talking to him is dangerous."

"Carlos." Harvey grinned, closing the folder in front of him. "That's just how I like it."

CHAPTER 5

"New tattoo?"

Lifting the sleeve of his black t-shirt, Private Investigator Jack Grayson revealed the new tattoo on his left shoulder. "Got it last week. It's always been my life motto, 'No regrets'."

"I really hope that in twenty years' time, when the tattoo removal person is using a laser to burn that off, they see the irony of that tattoo."

"Ha!" Jack slapped his hand down on the table, laughing heartily. "I was going to get a tattoo that said 'No Fear' across my back, but the thought of it hurting scared me too much."

This time, it was Harvey's turn to laugh loudly. "The tattoo I love the best is one that says, 'Trust No One' because unless you put that on yourself, then you had to trust someone."

Jack laughed loudly again. The two chuckling men in the small café captured all the other customers' attention. Jack Grayson was used to the attention. When he walked into a room, most heads turned.

The café was narrow and busy, filled with office workers looking for a moment of escapism. The smell of freshly roasted coffee filled the air, almost strong enough for a customer to consume a caffeine hit on the smell alone. The lighting was dim enough to provide a contrast to the sunshine outside, and the air-conditioning was working overtime to keep the place cool.

"I was at a restaurant last night, and the waitress screamed, 'Anyone know CPR?' I yelled out, 'Yeah, I know the whole alphabet,' and everyone laughed... well, except that one guy."

"That's a good joke." Harvey laughed again. "But is that a touch of gray hair I see?" Harvey tilted his head to inspect the first few strands of gray on Jack's head. "You need to dye that hair, or somebody might start taking you seriously."

"Don't even start, Harvey." Jack ran his hand over his temple, brushing over his short black hair. "I saw a few strands the other day, but I've never used hair dye in my life. I wouldn't even know how to use it."

"It's pretty simple. Just go to the drug store, buy a packet of hair dye, and follow the instructions on the box."

"I'm not good at following instructions. You know that."

"That's true. You should go and see a professional. Don't do it yourself. I would hate to see you walk in here next week with half your face dyed a different color."

"I need to protect this face. It's all I've got. You've got your smarts and your money; all I have is this pretty little smile." Jack grinned as he tried to find a comfortable position on the wooden chair.

The café chair wasn't big enough for him. Most chairs weren't. As a six-foot-four, broad, and muscular man, Jack Grayson filled most things out.

Including his T-shirt.

But then, if he didn't buy his t-shirts two sizes too

small, they wouldn't be as tight around his biceps.

"You've had more than your fair share of women." Harvey made the obvious understatement. "Give the rest of the male population a chance for once."

The twenty-something waitress placed two coffees in front of them, never quite taking her eye off Jack Grayson. With his square jaw, healthy skin, and mesmerizing blue eyes, Harvey was used to getting female attention, but when Jack was in the room, he didn't stand a chance. Confidently, Jack winked at the girl and watched her walk away with a spring in her step.

"OK, Harvey, what have you got for me?" He swirled the coffee in his mug.

"As you probably know, Judge Andrew Hardgrave was murdered a month ago."

"I read that in the news. He was your mentor, wasn't he?"

"He was. A great man. We met ten years ago when I was a baby-faced lawyer, and he took me under his wing. I didn't have much of an idea of what I was doing, but he showed me the ropes. I think he saw a lot of himself in me, and he could see that I wanted to make a difference. We met so many times, and I learned so much from him. Plus, we got along really well on a personal level. We were good friends. We had the same sense of humor."

"None?"

Harvey smiled. "What's the difference between a snowman and a snowwoman?"

"What?" Jack started to laugh.

"Snowballs."

"Ha!" Jack laughed hard, slapping his hand back

on the flimsy wooden table. If he hit it too much harder, it would crumble under the weight of his large hands.

"That was Hardgrave's favorite joke. He told it to me every year after he came back from his annual ski trip in Canada. He always had tears in his eyes when he tried to tell that joke."

"It's a good one." Jack calmed down, still chuckling slightly.

"We used to have dinner once a month, and Mary would cook the greatest turkey in the world. Oh, that was good turkey. I've never had better. Mary was his second wife; his first wife died of cancer over a decade ago. Hardgrave told me that he'd done a lot of things in his past that he wasn't proud of, but he was determined to redeem himself. He tried hard to make a difference in the world."

"And no one has been arrested for his murder yet?"

"Not yet."

"What have the police got?"

"A connection to my client, Carlos López."

"Really? And you're still defending him?"

"I have to keep him close. He's a reformed drug addict who spends all his time volunteering at a drug rehab center, but who knows what happened. The closer I am to López, the closer I am to the Hardgrave case. I won't let Hardgrave's case go cold. I won't let my friend's killer walk free."

"What's in the López case?"

"Drug possession charges. A briefcase full of heroin was found in his apartment when the cops raided it."

"Why were the cops raiding the place?"

"The apartment that Carlos lives in is owned by his cousin, Juan Lewis, and—"

"The drug dealer?"

"You know him?"

"Of course I do. Everyone around East L.A. knows him. His reputation is about as big as they come in those parts. He's rich, he's mean, and he loves women."

"Along with Hardgrave's daughter, apparently. Lewis and Michelle Hardgrave were an on-and-off item for many years. That's how Hardgrave is connected to Lewis."

"Why were there drugs in López's house if he's clean?"

"He claims that the cops planted the drugs. He claims that the police were trying to set up Lewis and take him down. Lewis and López were supposed to be in the apartment at the time of the raid, but they'd slipped out the laundry room window an hour earlier."

"Why?"

"I don't know yet, but I'm working on figuring that out."

"And if the police did plant the drugs, why plant them at López's place? Why not Lewis' house?"

"Lewis spends a lot of time at the apartment, and the cops thought it was one of his drug houses. It wasn't."

"Well, they messed that up." Jack groaned. "And so, you want me to look at Carlos' business? Get the inside word to see if he's still involved in the drug trade?"

"No. I don't think the briefcase full of drugs belonged to him. I feel he's telling the truth when he says he'd never seen that briefcase before. What I want from you is to sniff around Juan Lewis and Roberto Miles. See how deep their connections to Hardgrave go. See what the word is on them."

"You want me to be hunting around the case with Judge Hardgrave? Not working the López case?"

"There isn't a lot we can do with the López case. It's fairly black and white. We'll only be able to get him off on a technicality or if he makes a deal with the prosecution to sell out Lewis or Miles."

"He won't do that. Lewis and Roberto Miles are both dangerous men, and you would have to be crazy to try and cross them. I don't think for a second that anyone is going to cross Lewis or Miles. Nobody would be that stupid. It would be far better to do prison time than cross them."

"Then the answer is yes—I want you to look into the Hardgrave case. See what you can uncover. Do you have much on?"

"Not a thing. Work's drying up. Most people do their investigations online these days. An hour on Facebook could tell you more than a week's worth of following someone."

"I don't have a Facebook account, so I'm going to need you." Harvey handed a folder to Jack. "But this is going to get heavy. These guys are dangerous, so I need you to remember what your tattoo says, 'No Fear'. That's how I want you to go into this one."

"But I didn't get that tattoo. I chose the other one that said, 'No Regrets.'"

"Really? I don't think that was the right choice." The smile on Harvey's face grew. "You should've chosen the other one. I bet you'll regret that decision one day."

CHAPTER 6

The smell of Mexican spices and overcooked meat filled the air.

Bill Harvey caught a waft of the cooking, and his stomach instantly rumbled. He loved that smell. It reminded him of when he'd first moved into a small apartment in Downtown L.A., and his neighbors had cooked all afternoon and then fought all night. When he was missing his hometown, the nightly routine had comforted him.

Walking into the El Mejor diner, which Lewis and Carlos were known to frequent, Bill Harvey placed his hat on the bench, cautiously sitting on a sticky and squeaky stool.

He always thought it was odd where people felt most comfortable. Despite the ability to afford even the most high-end restaurants in town, Juan Lewis spent most of his time at a diner where all the meals were under ten dollars. It was cramped, the tables weren't cleaned properly, and there were ten-year-old coffee cup stains on the counter. The radio was humming in the background; the chatter of the locals was constant.

But this was more than just another diner serving Mexican food.

This was a community. A place where people felt

safe to be themselves.

That should never be underrated.

"What'll it be?" The woman behind the counter had a clear Mexican accent and a cheeky grin. Her round cheeks glowed, her eyes smiling at her new customer.

"This is a nice diner." He looked around. "What've got?"

"It's a Mexican diner, sweetheart. If you want hotdogs and bacon, go around the corner to a place called Dogs and Hots. You'll only find good Mexican food here."

"Let's start with coffee before we make this a date."

"Smooth and handsome." She grinned. "I like you. You've already added a little bit of sunshine to my day."

She poured the drip coffee into a mostly white mug without taking her eyes off his.

"Tell me…" He read the nametag on the lady's large chest. "Louise, what do you know about Carlos López?"

"Carlos? Why are you asking about Carlos?"

"I understand he comes here a lot."

"That might be correct, but you didn't answer my question."

"Do you spend a lot of time here, Louise?"

"Work is my life, mister. I spend all my time here. This is where people respect me, and I feel comfortable. Out those doors, I'm just another overweight Mexican woman. In here, I'm the woman everyone wants to talk to. I'm the center of a community here. This is where I'm somebody."

"You've worked here for a long time?"

"Years and years. This is all I know. I wouldn't know how to spend my time outside of work. And I don't like spending time in my own head. Too many crazy thoughts up there. I'm always being told to take holidays, but I'm not going to leave this place. It defines who I am."

"If you spend a lot of time here, then you would know Carlos López."

"But like I said, mister, you haven't answered my question."

Harvey drew a long sip of his lukewarm coffee, avoiding the temptation to spit it back out. He drummed his fingers gently on the counter, looked around to check that nobody was listening to their conversation, and then looked Louise straight in the eyes. "I'm his attorney, and he's in some trouble."

"Why didn't you say so?" She smiled. "If you're a friend of Carlos, then you're a friend of ours. Yeah, we all know Carlos. Known him for years. He comes in here a few times every week. Usually orders the beef taco. He's a good man. A very good man. He's done a lot—helped people with drug problems. He works down at the rehab center, and he helped my cousin kick the drugs. Carlos is a very good man. Almost a saint."

"Is he ever involved in trouble?"

"Carlos?" She pondered. "No, Carlos isn't trouble. Never."

"But?"

"But the people he spends time with are trouble."

"Like who?"

Louise leaned forward on the counter, squeezing her breasts together. It caught Harvey's eye, and she felt happy about that.

"You didn't hear this from me." Her voice was low. "Juan Lewis. Roberto Miles. Now both those men are trouble. Lewis especially. He looks mighty fine and dresses really well, but he's trouble. Always has been. He has a collection of the best suits, but the only way he can afford them is to break the law. He's the brains behind a lot of the crime that happens around here—money laundering, drugs, illegal gambling... but you didn't hear any of this information from me."

"Of course not, Louise."

He looked into the eyes of the woman and saw a lost soul. Her shoulders were tight, her eyes had a tinge of yellow from too much vodka every night, and her hands shook a little as she held the coffee server. She was searching for something, but she was looking for it externally, blaming others for her pain when the source of all her hurt was inside her.

"Do you have a husband, Louise?" Harvey asked, attempting to charm her.

"No, sir."

"I find that surprising." He smiled. "You have very beautiful eyes."

"Mister, flattery will get you everywhere."

"Then tell me how often you see Lewis and Carlos in here together."

"Every week. They're always here talking about something. Talking, talking, talking. I don't listen to their conversations, but they come every week. They know all of the people around these parts."

"How about on September 12? Were they here that day?"

"How would I know? That was a month ago, and I'm not a superwoman. I don't have a super memory.

Mister, I struggle to remember what color bra I put on in the mornings."

"You certainly present yourself as a superwoman, Louise. I'm sure a lot of people here actually believe that you are." Harvey smiled.

"Looks can be deceiving."

"Yes, they can. But if you can't remember that day, then maybe there's surveillance footage of that time?"

"You're smooth, Mister Attorney." She grinned. "Let me check with the boss."

The voluptuous waitress disappeared out the back of the diner, and Harvey overheard a loud argument between Louise and her boss. She returned with a calm smile on her face.

"My boss is more than happy for you to have a look at the footage… if, of course, you leave a large tip for the service."

Smoothly, Harvey placed a hundred-dollar bill next to his cold coffee.

"That should cover it." She smiled again. "Follow me this way."

The office at the back of the diner was exactly what he expected—small, confined, piles of old paperwork about to topple over. Kate Spencer would have a heart attack if she had to work in this office. The smell of cigarette smoke filled the air, drowning out the smell of Mexican spices cooking only a few feet away.

The older man sitting behind a cramped desk didn't greet Harvey as he entered. He didn't even stop staring at the computer in front of him.

"September 12?" the man questioned.

"Yes."

"Here it is." The man turned the computer screen

to face Harvey without a hint of emotion.

Harvey studied the footage, scrolling through it at a reasonable pace but not fast enough to miss anything important. The tape started at ten in the morning and finished at ten at night. With the advantage of technology, he was able to scroll through the twelve hours of footage in under a few minutes.

"This is the whole day?" Harvey asked when the video finished.

"Yes."

"I need a copy of this." Harvey placed another hundred on the table in front of the stern man.

The boss nodded and then shouted loudly, "Give me a USB, Louise."

Louise reappeared—having gotten used to her boss' bellows from the back room. She found a USB drive in the drawers, and the man placed the drive in the computer, punched his keyboard aggressively, and then removed it to hand to Harvey.

"Has anyone else asked about the footage from that day?"

"No." The old man shook his head.

"If anyone else requests this file, then I need to know. You need to call me; do you understand?"

The man gestured to the hundred-dollar bill Harvey put on the table.

"Of course." Harvey removed another hundred from his wallet. Sometimes, information costs a lot.

Placing the USB in his jacket pocket, Harvey offered Louise a nod, then walked tall out of the diner, leaving his nauseating coffee behind. It was not often he spent three hundred dollars in a small diner, but he hoped this information would be more fulfilling than a large burrito.

As soon as he stepped onto the sidewalk, he called his secretary. "Kate, I need Carlos in my office. Now."

CHAPTER 7

Carlos fidgeted, rubbing his thumbs together while waiting for his lawyer. He sat in the chair opposite Harvey's large desk, his head down, staring at the floor like a schoolboy waiting for the principal.

"I want the truth." Harvey stormed into the office. "No more lies."

"I'm not sure what you're talking about?" His answer was honest, but only because he had too many lies to protect.

"Tell me where you were when they raided your apartment on September 12."

With an aggressive overtone, Harvey's briefcase slapped down onto the office table, and he huffed into a chair, leaning forward, resting his thick arms on the desk.

"I was at the El Mejor diner. I was having lunch with Juan Lewis when they raided my apartment. We had the beef taco and a few coffees. That's what I told the police when they arrested me, and that's what I'm telling you."

"How about you tell me the truth instead."

"What do you mean?"

"If this is going to work, then you and I are going to have to be honest with one another. I have seen the security footage of the diner for that day, and neither you nor Lewis were in the diner at the time, or at any time during that day. Where were you?"

"The diner has security footage?" Carlos was surprised. "That place has nothing worth protecting. Why would they have security footage?"

"Lucky for us, nobody else, including the prosecution, has checked if the diner has security footage. They seem to think that it's not important where you were at the time of the raid. They haven't checked your alibi. They're only concerned with the fact that they found the drugs in your apartment."

"If they don't think it's important, then why do you think it's important?"

"The truth is important to me, Carlos."

"Look, I can't remember where I was at the time."

"Is it best that I speak to Lewis about this?"

Carlos paused and looked to make sure the door was shut behind him. "We're still covered by the attorney-client agreement, aren't we?"

Harvey nodded slowly, not taking his eyes off Carlos.

"OK. Sure. Look, Lewis came to me and said that he needed an alibi for the day. I agreed that I would help him. He came to the apartment, and we both slipped out the side exit."

"Then where were you all day?"

"I was driving around."

"Why?"

"I couldn't be seen anywhere. I had to make sure that I wasn't seen on any surveillance footage. So, I drove to the State Forest in a friend's car and just drove the roads for most of the day. I left my car near the apartment."

"And Lewis?"

"I don't know where he was. I dropped him off,

and I picked him up four hours later. He went off to conduct a 'business transaction' and called me after lunch—told me that the time had passed and we could go back to my apartment. The problem was, when we came back, the police were crawling all over my apartment. Suddenly, he was as much my alibi as I was his."

"Why did he need an alibi?"

"I didn't ask. I never do."

"This is a common occurrence?" Despite spending the last ten years within smelling distance of criminal activity, the world of drug runs and organized crime still surprised Harvey.

"I've done it before, but it's not common. He usually walks into my apartment, we have a coffee, and then we sneak out via the laundry room window. Usually, we say that we were at my apartment all day. It's never been tested before. But this time, we couldn't say that we were at the apartment because it was filled with cops."

"Why didn't you stay at the apartment? Why did you have to leave?"

"I was the driver. We always use a friend's car that has dark-tinted windows. I had to drop Lewis off and pick him up."

"Where did you drop him off?"

"I dropped him off at a Taco Bell downtown and picked him up there four hours later."

"Four hours is a long time to spend at Taco Bell. So tell me where he really went."

"I never know why he needs an alibi, and I never ask. I don't want to know. All I'm doing is helping out my cousin, which is my family duty. We look after each other. He helps me out with cash, and I help him out as long as I'm not doing anything criminal."

"With cash?"

Carlos shrugged, uncomfortable with the notion. "I don't have a paying job. All my time is spent at the rehab center. Lewis… he supports me when I need it. I have savings that I invested, but for day-to-day things, he helps me out."

"What about your lawyer? Is he paying for that too?"

"No." Carlos coughed loudly. "My savings are paying your wages."

Harvey paused, letting the tension in the room dissipate. He opened his briefcase, removed his notes, and reviewed them before he continued. "What do you think Lewis was doing during the time you dropped him off?"

"I don't think about it."

"So when did you make the decision to say that you were at the diner?"

"When we drove back to my apartment. We could see all the cop cars out front. We couldn't say that we were in the apartment; we had to use another destination. That's why we chose the diner. We're always there, and nobody would remember which day was which. We didn't think they would have security footage."

Harvey scribbled more notes, trying to piece together the picture of September 12. He had no doubt that Carlos was telling the truth, but he was no closer to winning the case that threatened the freedom of a reformed drug addict.

"It must be painful for you, Carlos. You spend your time working in drug rehabilitation, helping people recover, and your cousin is the person putting people in there. He's the one that's dealing drugs, and you have to clean up his mess. That must hurt you on some level."

"Personal choice causes addiction. Loneliness. Emptiness. Being hollow causes addiction. Not Lewis. Just because the drugs are there doesn't mean that someone has to take them. You don't blame the shopkeepers for alcoholism, just like you don't blame the drug dealers for the addiction. It's a personal decision."

"And yet, you have enormous guilt around your involvement in the drug trade."

Carlos fumbled his hand through his pocket, reaching for more cigarettes. "I guess I try to justify what Lewis does. I know the truth, but if the police can't stop him, how am I supposed to? I love the man, but he deals in death."

Harvey flicked open a paper file, his eyes searching through the notes.

"Lewis' rap sheet is clean. He has never been charged with any criminal offense and has never even been taken in by the police. He's either very good, very smart, or very lucky."

"He's all three. His father was a dealer and taught him everything he knew. He has always been well-connected, even before he met Hardgrave."

"Where does he get the drugs?"

Carlos paused, thinking about how much information he could divulge. "I…"

"I want the whole truth, Carlos."

He nodded. "The drugs are produced in a small lab in Mexico, smuggled over the border, and then run through the streets. Lewis and Roberto Miles run the operations, and they're worth millions. Many millions. They don't get their hands dirty, though. They're at the top of the tree, and they avoid dealing with anyone they don't know."

"And you? What's your involvement in it? Where do you fit into the Lewis business puzzle?"

"I used to run the labs in Mexico. I would fly down once every two weeks to make sure everything was working fine. It was just a job to me, although I was well paid by Lewis. I saved enough money to get out of the game. Now, Lewis and I are just family rather than business associates. I keep telling him to get out of the game while he's ahead, but he likes the money. He has dreams of becoming big. Real big. I keep telling him that the bigger he gets, the bigger the target grows on his back, but he doesn't want to hear it. He thinks he's invincible."

"It appears he still is," Harvey said as he started to write notes on his pad. "How deep was your involvement in the drug dealing?"

"I managed the labs that produced the gear." Carlos nodded. "I never stood on a street corner and dealt drugs. No. I had nothing to do with that side of things. I was only responsible for making sure the gear was good and that the people in Mexico were playing nicely."

"But you knew that the labs were producing drugs?"

"Of course."

"Tell me how Lewis has made all his high-profile connections."

"He was always just one of those people that knew people. Local people, though. But it all started to get big when he began dating Judge Hardgrave's daughter, Michelle. He hassled the judge a lot. He got a lot of information from the judge just through extortion. I think he was using Michelle, in the end, to keep close to the judge. And because of Judge Hardgrave, he met with numerous high-ranking police officers and politicians."

"Did he love her, or was he just using her?"

"He loved her. Deeply. She's a troubled woman with a long addiction to drugs, and she was estranged from her father for many years. Lewis reconnected them after they hadn't talked for a long time. And Michelle, being a drug addict, would do anything for Lewis. So, he started setting up regular meetings between the two of them. A father's love for his daughter can make a man do very strange things. I think the judge was just happy to have a chance with his daughter again, and he would do anything to keep that connection. Of course, Judge Hardgrave was a wealthy man, and that meant that Michelle was going to inherit a lot of money."

"So Lewis would have profited from Hardgrave's death?"

"Through Michelle, yes."

The pen hovered over the pad, stuck as the thoughts raced through Harvey's head. "Carlos, the further we get into these cases, the more Lewis seems to be involved. The more Lewis gets involved, the more this case is going to escalate. You've given the police a sworn statement of your whereabouts at the time of the raid, so we can't change that, but it's going to be a sticking point for the prosecution. I'm going to consider our options, but in the meantime, I need you to stay away from Lewis. Understood?"

"Sure."

"Good." Harvey closed the file in front of him.

"We're done for now, but I don't want any more falsehoods."

"Yes, sir." Carlos bowed his head, then stood to leave the room. "When will I hear from you again?"

"Within the week. Kate will call you and set up a time to meet."

After Carlos had closed the door behind him, Harvey paced the floor in his office, reflecting on the two cases before him. Hardgrave had mentioned his daughter and her addiction. He blamed himself for it, and it seemed rightly so.

On a rare night when Judge Hardgrave had consumed too much fine whiskey, he would open up about his troubled past.

He had been beaten weekly by his drunken father as a child and had carried that pain into his first marriage. Despite the joy of having a loving wife, a beautiful daughter, and a great career, he would come home drunk most nights of the week and beat his wife, often in full view of a young Michelle.

After years of torment, Hardgrave's first wife died a lonely death following a short battle with cancer.

At the time of her mother's death, Michelle was a troubled sixteen-year-old, and she left the family home, wrongly blaming her father for her mother's death. She found comfort in the highs that drugs provided. That's when her path crossed with Juan Lewis. She knew if she were close to him, she wouldn't have to buy drugs. She could provide him the comfort that he needed, and he would give her the highs that she desperately craved.

The remorse that Andrew Hardgrave suffered was clear. He acknowledged that it was all his fault and that he had ruined Michelle's young life. When at his worst, he turned to A.A. for help. He went to rehab and came out wanting to redeem himself.

It took years, but he started to turn his life around.

He volunteered at schools, donated a lot of his wealth to the disadvantaged, and mentored people to do positive things in the world. When Andrew Hardgrave and Bill Harvey first met, they felt like kindred spirits. They wanted to make a difference. They wanted to leave the world a better one than the one they were born into.

The Harvey family was no stranger to drug addiction, either. Harvey's younger brother, Jonathon, had gone missing twenty years ago after becoming addicted to heroin. It had been a painful journey. Jonathon stole from his family, lashed out at his parents, and constantly swore at everyone. His descent into addiction almost tore the family apart.

When Jonathon lashed out and hit his mother, Harvey had finally taken matters into his own hands. He beat Jonathon, brutally, and told him never to return.

That was twenty years ago, and nobody had seen him since.

It was still Harvey's greatest heartache.

He understood the pain that Hardgrave felt when watching his daughter wither away—he had felt the same pain with his brother.

Harvey had searched for his lost brother for many years but never found a trace of him. He thought he had a lead in Florida, but that turned out to be a dead end. Now, all he hoped was that his brother was well and had won the battle against addiction.

If he could see his brother one more time, just for a moment, he would say everything that had been left unsaid and ask for forgiveness.

Andrew Hardgrave would never have that chance with his daughter.

CHAPTER 8

Roberto Miles walked out of his Montebello house just past seven.

He looked like the wealthy man he was. Rolex watch. Ralph Lauren shirt. Armani slacks. Ferragamo shoes. He walked with his head held high, full of confidence and bravado. He didn't go far.

His black Audi was parked on the sidewalk near his house. Perfectly matching his outfit.

Despite the obvious trimmings of excess wealth, Roberto Miles was a man with a long criminal record. Whereas Juan Lewis had always escaped the clutches of the law, Roberto knew police officers by their first name. If the police printed his rap sheet, they would need to change the roll of paper on the printer halfway through.

Bill Harvey didn't have much to go on. Nobody on the streets talked about these men. Those who knew Roberto Miles and Juan Lewis also knew what they could do. Their digital footprint was as non-existent as the word on the street. They weren't interested in splashing themselves across social media. They had no need to tell everyone how rich they were—everyone already knew that.

There was no easy method for gathering information on Miles or Lewis. Finding information about them involved old-fashioned investigative work. The hard yards.

Harvey followed the Audi as it drove for an hour, staying two to three cars behind, trying to go unnoticed.

The Audi parked on Rodeo Drive, double-parked outside a bar, the sort of place where old rich men buy drinks for beautiful young women.

Harvey found a spot further down the street to park and made his way back to the bar. He had no idea what he was going to find. More than likely, Miles was just meeting someone for a drink and looking to have his ego boosted by an attractive, young, gold-digging woman. Still, it was worth a shot to see the sort of circles that Miles floated in.

The bar was packed, the crowd mingling freely with each other, making it hard to spot Miles and who he was meeting. The dim lighting didn't help, either.

Harvey pulled out his phone for two reasons. One, if he needed to duck his head to avoid detection, he could look down at his phone quickly, and two, the camera on the smartphone made it easier to snap a quick picture.

He looked through the crowd from just inside the door and couldn't see Miles on the first pass.

Looking back down at his phone, he pretended to read an email, looking as if he was waiting for a friend as he leaned against one of the walls. Nothing unusual.

When he gazed up from his phone, he caught sight of the tall Mexican seated at the opposite end of the bar.

He was talking to someone. Quietly. Tactfully.

This wasn't a loud conversation that he wanted people to hear.

This was discreet and deliberate.

Nobody from his East L.A. drug operation would risk being seen there. This was a secret meeting in public. Harvey moved between two other businessmen, trying to get a better vantage point to see who Miles was talking to.

He moved to his left to get a better angle, to get a clear view of the person.

Moving smoothly, he shot a glance at the end of the bar.

What?

He looked again.

Harvey's heart kicked into overdrive. He couldn't believe what he had just seen.

Maybe it was the dim lighting. Maybe he was mistaken.

He looked again, holding the stare.

Dim lighting, crowded or not, he hadn't made a mistake.

Roberto Miles was quietly swapping information with a detective.

A detective Harvey knew very well.

CHAPTER 9

Harvey worked his way through the crowd, past the throng of people desperate to get noticed. He stepped into the sunshine, his vision taking a few moments to adapt.

The question buzzed through his head.

What was Pitt doing? That wasn't a formal meeting. Not a police interview.

It was a quiet discussion with a possible suspect in the unsolved Judge Hardgrave murder case. Was Pitt an inside man for Miles, screwing the force? Screwing justice?

Surely not. Not his friend. Harvey knew how to read people, and nobody could play him that well. If Pitt were dirty, he would know. Wouldn't he?

The doubt grew easily in his mind. What had he missed? What had he not seen?

Harvey walked to his car in a fog of thoughts, sat in the driver's seat, and drew a long, deep breath.

Was this why Hardgrave's killer hadn't been charged?

Was there a dirty cop protecting them all?

This was the biggest murder case of the year, and the LAPD hadn't even made an arrest. They hadn't even presented a suspect to the public.

Something in the murder case wasn't right. Something was wrong.

Harvey had known Pitt for many years. Their friendship was strong, and their trust was stronger.

But Pitt had just bought a new house. Larger. Nicer. A good suburb. "My share investments went up," he'd said. He had just returned from a luxury cruise through parts of Europe. "I sold some shares," he'd said.

And maybe that was true.

Or maybe he was taking payments from somewhere else.

Despite Harvey's great respect for the men and women in blue, most of the force hated Bill Harvey. That was understandable. His job was to make their arrests look invalid, their evidence look shoddy, or their paperwork look incomplete. While they risked their lives to protect justice on a small wage, he argued in a courtroom for a nice paycheck. He understood their resentment.

But Pitt was different.

Harvey had a bond with Pitt, one that went beyond their jobs.

He had first met Pitt when he graduated as a lawyer—a chance meeting in an L.A. dive bar. Pitt was fascinated by Harvey's previous job as a hypnotherapist, and their bond was instant. They joked, they laughed, and they drank. The perfect male companions.

Even as their careers progressed, they'd joined each other every week for a Tuesday after-work drink.

But maybe it wasn't a coincidence.

Maybe Pitt had played him from the start. Maybe Pitt had heard of Harvey's skills and sought to exploit them. There had certainly been occasions where

Harvey had shared more than what was needed.

But the exchange generally went both ways.

Pitt shared the information that Harvey required. Nothing unlawful, only a gentle nudge in the right direction. It was a good professional partnership, as much as it was an escape from their jobs.

But it was more than that.

It was a genuine bond. A real connection. Two men trying to do their best for themselves and their community.

But now Bill Harvey had to test that bond and find out how close Pitt was playing to the line.

CHAPTER 10

The lighting in the bar was dim, as was the atmosphere. The floor was sticky, the tables dirty, and the shelves were filled with cheap spirits. The only noise came from the two televisions at the end of the bar; one was playing baseball, and the other was playing college football.

Bill Harvey was comfortable drinking alone, staring into his whiskey, thinking about nothing in particular. It was only once the soft touch of Kate's hand rested on his shoulder that he was brought back to reality.

"Kate?" he asked in slight surprise. "How did you know I was here?"

"You had that look in your eyes when you left the office. The last time I saw that look, you stumbled back into the office six hours later stinking of whiskey."

He remembered that moment. He had been told that one of his former clients had committed suicide—too ashamed that they had been tarnished with the guilty brush. He had told his client, Jessica Tate Wilson, to take a deal, even though she was protesting her innocence. The deal involved a fine for minor theft but no criminal record. He thought the deal was the best option. If the case had gone to court, Jessica would have been charged. There was evidence that she'd stolen from Walmart, but she claimed it was all a mistake. She took the deal, and her very religious family found out. They didn't want to be associated with a criminal. They abandoned her.

Harvey had felt responsible for the woman's fate. He felt it was his fault that her life fell apart. When he returned to the office, he was drunk, vulnerable, and lonely.

That was the moment when he'd almost told Kate how he felt about her.

Almost.

"What's up?" Kate playfully punched him in the arm, like a little sister teasing her tough brother.

"Jonathon." Harvey stared into his glass. The name came out of his mouth before he had the chance to think about what he was saying.

"Your brother?" She sounded surprised.

This wasn't the first time that he had mentioned his brother to Kate, but she hadn't heard his name in a long time. Jonathon had played on Harvey's mind his whole life, and he didn't know how to fix it.

Bill Harvey knew how to fix most things, but there was one thing he couldn't fix, one thing that was beyond his capability: his family.

His late wife had talked about having children in the future, but he had balked at the idea. When she was first diagnosed with cancer five years ago, he'd felt guilty for not giving her the family she wanted. A year later, he was burying the only family he'd ever felt really comfortable with.

Although his early childhood in a small farming community was pleasant, the years since have brought him nothing but heartache. His brother, Jonathon, younger by eight years, became addicted to drugs in his late teens. It was a rollercoaster ride, and not a fun one. His entire family was devastated as they watched the high school quarterback slowly fall into a world of pain and anguish.

It had torn them apart.

They tried everything. Everything.

Counselors. Friends. Psychologists. Locking him in his room. Moving towns. Nothing stopped Jonathon's need for heroin. Nothing stopped his need for another high.

It had hit his father the hardest. It was his greatest failing as a man.

His distant father, whom Harvey adored, decided one morning to eat a bullet for breakfast, and his dear mother never recovered.

"Michelle Hardgrave, the judge's daughter, was estranged from her father for years. She was battling a drug addiction. That triggered memories of Jonathon for me." Harvey swirled the whiskey in his glass, the ice clinking on the sides. "The drugs, the turmoil, the chaos. It all comes flooding back. The fear in Jonathon's eyes when he was so far into addiction, that will never leave me. And I can't stand it, Kate. I should be able to leave it in the past, but I can't stop thinking about him."

"And so you thought you could stay in a bar all night, and that would help?"

"It usually does."

"You can't keep doing this, Bill. One day, you'll have to face your emotions. Otherwise, they'll just keep coming back, worse and worse each time."

Harvey shrugged his shoulders. Like his father, he refused to get drawn into emotional conversations.

"We all have our past. Even Judge Hardgrave made a lot of mistakes."

"Don't change the subject, Bill," Kate replied. "This is about you, not Hardgrave."

He shook his head, whispering quietly into his glass. "I'm not ready to talk about it."

In silence, they sat at the bar, the thoughts racing through their heads.

When many minutes of silence had passed, Kate redirected the conversation back to work, back to the topic that made Harvey feel most comfortable.

"Hardgrave didn't seem like the type of person that would be estranged from his daughter," Kate added. "He seemed like such a nice guy. He was always so lovely to me when he came into the office. Very charming and sweet for an old man."

"That's the Hardgrave we knew, but he was not the same man in the past. He spent the last ten years of his life working for redemption, and he genuinely wanted to do better in the world. He wanted to make a difference. But he was another man once."

"How so?"

"He used to beat his first wife. Regularly." Harvey sighed. "Michelle witnessed that and abandoned him after her mother died of cancer. Hardgrave and his daughter didn't speak for another five years."

"Oh." Kate pointed at the beer tap when the bartender raised his eyebrows at her. "I wouldn't have guessed that, Bill. I can hardly imagine that. He seemed like such a calm soul, but I guess you never know what happens behind closed doors."

"He meditated a lot in his later years. That's why he seemed so calm. I guess his first wife would have loved to have seen him meditating years ago. People change, Kate. Times change. Hardgrave certainly changed. But Michelle never saw the change in her father. She only remembered the mean, violent, abusive man that he once was. She only remembered the man that would come home drunk and abuse his wife and child."

"And that's fair," Kate said. "You can't just swipe a slate clean after it has been severely stained. Some stains are so deep, so ingrained, that no amount of scrubbing can get rid of them. Michelle's formative years were spent with a violent man; she couldn't forget that. I understand that. I guess some people can't recognize redemption in others, no matter how hard they try."

Harvey wanted to argue with Kate, but he knew she was probably right. She always was. Instead of arguing, he stared into the glass, tilting it until the large block of ice cube moved from the side.

The bartender placed a pint of pale ale in front of Kate, and she smiled joyfully. She slurped the head of the beer like a kid with a frosty from Wendy's.

"Remind me not to invite you to the pub again." Harvey chuckled as she licked her foam mustache away with her tongue.

"Want to hear a joke, Bill?" Kate said and then chugged down half of her beer. Just when Harvey thought she was about to take a breath, she kept going.

He had no doubt that she would have been a legend at any college she went to—if she had decided to go. There would have been posters of her mythical beer-drinking ability on the walls of a UCLA sorority.

Once the beer was placed in front of her, Kate's demeanor had changed. Now, she didn't have to pretend to be classy or intelligent. She could just focus on drinking beer.

Her brothers all drank like it was going out of fashion, and she'd been the same as a teenager. She loved the taste of beer. But when she got older, she learned that classy girls weren't supposed to drink beer like the boys. Classy girls were supposed to sip cocktails, delicately giggling when a boy looked their way. She'd reluctantly taken on that persona, but when she was at a bar with a beer in her hand, the old Kate came out from hiding. The one who had grown up with four older brothers.

"What does the sign on an out-of-business brothel say?"

"Go on." Harvey began to smile.

"Beat it. We're closed."

"Ha!"

"You like that one, huh?" Kate laughed. "Well, what's the difference between a pregnant woman and a light bulb?"

"What?"

"You can unscrew a light bulb."

"Kate." Harvey laughed. "You completely change when you have a beer in your hand." He grinned, his troubles seemingly forgotten under the spell of Kate's bright white smile.

"You know…" She looked at the pint glass, already empty in her hand. "Every loaf of bread is a tragic story of grains that could have been beer but didn't make it."

"It wouldn't surprise me if you were a dirty old man in a past life."

"Probably the past three lives. I'm just a dirty old man stuck in a girl's body." She slammed the glass back on the bar, holding back a small little burp. She waved to the bartender to bring her another pint, and Harvey grinned, staring at his liquor.

"So, now that the mood has been lightened, tell me." Kate paused for another small burp. "What is the connection between the Mexican drug dealers and Judge Hardgrave?"

"Michelle. Juan Lewis is Michelle's boyfriend. They've been dating for years. From what I can gather, it's not a healthy relationship; it's based on drug use. Lewis used Michelle to make connections with Hardgrave, and then he used Hardgrave to get information about other people he could use. He's a drug dealer that has escaped charges for a very long time."

"He sounds like a very cunning man," Kate added. "And all this talk of drugs has you thinking about your brother?"

Sighing, Harvey looked at the other end of the bar, eager to avoid eye contact with the woman who knew him the best. "Yes."

"Where do you think he is now?"

"Jonathon? I don't know. I just hope he's doing well for himself. That's all I want to hear. I don't need a hug from him, I don't need his forgiveness, I just need to hear that he's doing fine. I just want to know that my little bro is doing well."

"With that strong Harvey blood, I'm sure he is."

"Maybe." Harvey shrugged. "And maybe not. But enough about lost souls, Kate. Let's solve this case quickly so I don't have to confront any more of these emotions."

He would much rather be in the thick of the action, knee-deep in investigation and adrenaline than have time to listen to the thoughts in his own head.

"What do you need me to do, Bill?" Kate asked, happy that she had dug Harvey out of his hole before he spent the rest of the night sitting on the same bar stool. Another beer was placed in front of Kate, and her eyes lit up again.

"There's not a lot you can—" Harvey grimaced as Kate gulped down half a pint in one motion. "There's not a lot you can do at the moment."

"Come on, Bill." She wiped her mouth with the back of her hand. "There must be something I can help with. Let me help you. I really want to."

"If you really want to, you can look into Michelle Hardgrave. Do a little bit of digging around, but don't get close to her. I imagine that she's dangerous, so don't confront her at all. Just ask around, search the Internet, that sort of thing. I want to find out how she spends her days, who she's close to, where her income comes from, that sort of thing."

"I'm on it, sir."

"But be careful, OK? She's a drug addict, and that means she's dangerous."

"Yes, boss," she replied with a cheeky grin. "What are you going to do?"

"I'm going to meet with the prosecution, and then I'm going to find out more about these drug dealers. They're the key to the López case and possibly the Hardgrave case. I have to get close enough to them to find out what they know."

"You must promise you will be careful as well, Bill." The joy left Kate's face. "They've killed before, and they could do it again. These men are dangerous drug dealers. Promise me you'll be cautious."

Harvey smiled again. "Yes, sir."

CHAPTER 11

As he walked through the corridors leading to the prosecutor's office, Bill Harvey's shoulders stiffened. He loved the pressure that came with the first meeting between opposing lawyers—the meeting that could make or break a case.

He didn't have to meet face-to-face with the prosecuting attorney, but he never missed the opportunity. He was looking for that one small crack in their armor, that one brief moment when they hesitated to answer a question, that one quick glance to the left to cover a lie. So many times, this initial meeting had allowed him to follow a line of investigation that he hadn't previously considered, a small detail that could change a case.

Conversely, the prosecution might sense Harvey's apprehension about answering a question, and it would allow them to pounce. He had to play the game well.

The risks were high—but so were the rewards.

Much the same way Harvey lived his life.

"Mr. Harvey, it's been a while," the prosecutor stood at the door, welcoming him into her clean, open office.

The large room was spotless. There was no dust, nothing out of place, and the wooden desk looked like it had been polished within an inch of its life. An antique leather couch sat to one side of the room, and law books lined the other side. The blinds were drawn, and the dull lighting gave the room a sense of calm.

"Miss Shannon Chettle. It's always a pleasure."

After attending law school together, Harvey and Shannon Chettle's paths had crossed in the courtroom numerous times. A feisty spirit with an energetic attitude, she had the ability to turn the case on its head with one well-placed statement.

Her exquisite use of the English language left many in awe. Despite being Chicago-born, she had spent her teenage years boarding at an exclusive school in London; the slight English accent was still noticeable and a little seductive.

"When was the last time I was up against you?" Chettle walked to the head of her desk, taking small steps in her tight pencil skirt, and opened a file on her laptop. Harvey sat in the dark leather chair in front of her desk.

"Shannon, I think the last time you were up against me was late on a Friday night after we settled on a case earlier that day…"

"Oh yes…" Chettle's mind drifted back to the last time she'd seen Harvey. She twirled her fingers through her long, dark hair as she remembered that passionate night three years ago. It was a moment of release, a moment of sexual tension and passion so fiery that it exploded into a mind-blowing night. "You look as formidable and as attractive as the last time I saw you, Bill. Age has been kind to you."

"And you're still as pretty." He smiled. "But that isn't what we're here to talk about."

"Ah, yes…" Chettle scrolled through the document on the computer screen. "The extraordinary trial of the innocent drug dealer. A briefcase full of drugs was found in his apartment, next to his bed, no less. A street value of $50,000, I hear. Of course, the drugs weren't his, were they?"

"That's what he said."

"And what do you think?"

"It doesn't matter what I think, Shannon. It only matters what happens in the courtroom. You must know that by now."

"I thought you could read people better than anyone else. You must have an opinion."

"I have an opinion."

"And please, feel free to share your opinion with me."

"My opinion is that you look beautiful."

"About the case." Chettle grinned and pushed a strand of brunette hair behind her ear.

"The case." Harvey sat back in his chair, crossed one leg over the other, and looked around the perfectly maintained office. Only a perfectionist could keep an office this organized. "I think the evidence is soft, I think the motives are questionable, and I think that the whole case is pathetic."

"Then you should ask yourself, why would we even bother with a flimsy case?" Chettle made eye contact. Her deep blue eyes were hypnotic, and Harvey struggled to maintain focus.

"We both know why you're pressing ahead with this case. You're after someone else. You're pushing my client into a corner and hoping that he breaks. Despite the fact that my client dedicates his time to helping those recovering from drug addiction, you want to use him to expose someone else's crime. This is a man who does good in the world, and you're willing to sacrifice his future to capture someone else. That's not justice."

"I'm afraid that I'm not completely sure what you're talking about." Chettle played the game.

"You're after Juan Lewis. You want to pressure Carlos until he cracks and then put him on the stand against Lewis. I can see that the cops even thought that Lewis was in the apartment when the raid occurred. My client is innocent. Let him walk away and continue to help others. Let him help people recover from their drug addiction."

"You must have read a different police report than the one I read because I didn't see that piece of information anywhere. Could you please point that out to me?"

"It's about reading between the lines. Of course, the police wouldn't admit to a mistake like that. But that's who they wanted. They wanted Lewis. My client is an innocent bystander. An innocent man."

"Your client has a history of drug convictions. He's not as innocent as you claim he is."

"Carlos did the time for those crimes, and that was ten years ago. He's out of the game and clean now. He's an innocent man, and he's been clean for years. He helps people; he doesn't destroy them. He's dedicated his life to helping others recover from the scourge of drugs."

"Innocent men don't get caught with a briefcase full of drugs in their apartment."

"And innocent cops don't plant briefcases full of drugs in people's apartments."

"Good luck proving that in court, Bill."

When Chettle had seen Bill Harvey's name on the defendant's notes, she was delighted. Her months were becoming a boring slog of case after case, charge after charge, late night after late night. To confront a man with Harvey's reputation in the courtroom invigorated her desire. It recharged her enthusiasm for the law. Today, for their first meeting, she was wearing her best suit, one that she had only bought a week before, and she'd added an extra spray of her best perfume.

It was having the desired effect on her opponent. She could see it in his eyes.

"You have a bigger office than the last time I saw you," Harvey stated, looking around the newly renovated space. "I see that you even have your name on the door."

"My career is on the up and up. I work hard, and I'm getting the rewards for that. The people here respect me, and I'm well-known throughout the department. That's what happens when you work hard."

"That must be nice," he quipped. "Tell me about one of the officers, Detective Matthew Pitt."

"Pitt? He wasn't the lead detective on this case."

"No, but he was present at the time of the raid. According to the police report, four detectives and four officers made the raid. Pitt was one of the detectives. Tell me about him."

"I'm not sure what you're asking?"

"Do you trust him?"

"Of course." Chettle's brows came together in confusion. "He's an outstanding officer and a good man. He's never had a problem. He's one of the good ones."

"Do you think he has any links to the case?"

"Other than the raid? No." Chettle shook her head.

"Nothing that Internal Affairs would know about?"

"No, Bill. Nothing."

Harvey uncrossed his legs and leaned his elbows on the large mahogany table. The table had been overly polished, so pristine that he could see his reflection in it.

"How about we just drop this case now and save ourselves some time? If you want Lewis, then go after him. Don't destroy an innocent man's reputation for the sake of one of his cousins. That's not what we got into law for. We got into law to uphold justice—and this isn't justice."

"This is about justice. Justice for the people on the street. The ones that have had their lives destroyed because of the drugs that are available to them. This is about cleaning up those streets for the children of the future. Carlos López is a drug dealer. He will do time. That's justice. And you know the deal that is on the table. Your client either provides information and testifies against Lewis, or we charge him."

"How much information do you need to strike a deal?"

"We need enough information to stop Lewis and his operations. It has to be enough so that we can charge Lewis with a crime that will do prison time. If the drugs belonged to Lewis, then we need your client to state that."

"You want him to testify in court?"

"That's right. Without the testimony from Mr. López that the drugs weren't his and belonged to Juan

Lewis, then we cannot let him walk away. That's the only deal that's on the table. Nothing else."

"Doesn't sound fair."

"Don't try and convince yourself that your client is innocent. I can guarantee you that he's not. He's not an innocent man. The only reason he spends time volunteering with drug addicts is because he feels guilty for all the pain and suffering he has caused in the past. Having his hands in the drug game hurt people. He hurt families. Destroyed them. He has a history of crime and has spent time behind bars. People don't change, Bill."

"People do change." Harvey's fist clenched. "Carlos has done his time for the crimes he committed, and it changed him. It changed his perspective. He's a good man now. And I won't let a good man go to prison for a crime that he hasn't committed."

"Don't believe the lies. Deep down, Carlos is still a drug dealer. He's still a criminal. It's in his blood."

"No." Harvey put his hand down heavily on the table, bringing a slight look of surprise from Chettle. "People do change. People redeem themselves. Carlos has done that. He did the wrong thing in the past and now spends his time making it right. He has changed. He has redeemed himself. And he shouldn't go to prison for something that he didn't do."

Chettle leaned back slightly, surprised to see such raw emotion from a man who was usually so measured. "You obviously feel very strongly about this."

"People can redeem themselves, Shannon."

"Maybe." She shrugged. "But if Carlos isn't going to give us what we want, then we're going to court."

"I will defend the innocent." Standing, Harvey placed his index finger down firmly on the table. "And I will make sure that an innocent man doesn't go to prison."

CHAPTER 12

Bill Harvey arrived at the Huntington Park coffee shop thirty minutes before his scheduled meeting.

He sat in a quiet corner, calming his thumping head with two Advil and two large coffees while turning his thoughts to his case.

The coffee shop was generic in its décor but edgy in its artwork. A black and white life-sized drawing of a naked woman—clearly the barista—hung on one wall, and a black and white photo of a half-naked man dressed in a skirt hung on the other wall. Edgy, but not quite offensive.

The coffee barely tickled Harvey's taste buds, but the warming liquid eased his throat. With his head down, trawling through emails on his phone, he was caught off guard by the arrival of Juan Lewis.

"Bill Harvey."

The man who approached was flamboyant in his walk, his clothes perfectly tailored, and he was immaculately groomed. His suit was navy blue, his shirt checkered pink, his tie bright orange. The style of his love heart necklace perfectly matched the three rings on his fingers.

Full of color, flair, and style.

Not what Harvey expected for a known drug dealer in East L.A.

They shook hands solidly, Harvey's large, strong hand dominating Lewis's. He was sure that Lewis wasn't dominated very often, but Harvey had to mark his territory. He had to show Lewis that he was the alpha male in this pack, ready to fight for the rights of his client. A strong handshake, a solid stare, and the odd grunt usually positioned Harvey at the head of the pack.

"How did you recognize me?" Harvey asked.

"I've seen you in the papers."

His last case had received a respectable write-up in all the papers. And a good write-up usually meant more business—but considering crime wasn't going out of fashion in L.A. any time soon, he wasn't too concerned about chasing media attention.

"That, and you're the only non-Mexican male around these parts."

Ten years ago, Harvey wouldn't have agreed to meet Lewis in Huntington Park for fear that he would be shot stepping out of his car, but the suburb had improved, and the community had worked hard to create a safer environment for their children.

With a sideways glance out the window, he saw a striking, restored 1960 red Chevy Impala. To drive that car around East L.A., his reputation must precede him.

"A 1960 Impala It's beautiful."

"Thank you," Lewis stated proudly, looking out at the car that he had just spent the last hour polishing. He sat at the table with confidence, waving at the barista to make him a coffee. "The car was my father's before he passed. Now, I take great pride in the beautiful machine."

Harvey took a moment longer to stare at the work

of art sitting on the side of the road.

"How is it that I can help you, Mr. Harvey?" Lewis slowly and confidently leaned back in his chair, legs spread wide, and arms relaxed.

"As you're aware, I'm defending Carlos López in the case of the drug—"

"They planted it." Lewis shook his hands in the air. "Carlos has been out of the game for a while now, and I would know if he was back in it. They weren't his drugs. I, of all people, would know if Carlos was dealing, but I can guarantee you that he wasn't. That man has no connection to dealing anymore. He's turned over a new leaf, a new life. He's out of the game. Even if he asked me, I wouldn't let him deal drugs again. He spends most of his time at the drug rehab center, so there is no way that the drugs were his. The cops planted it."

"Whether or not the drugs belonged to Carlos isn't the problem. It's whether or not we can prove in a court of law that the drugs weren't his."

Lewis laughed brashly, loud enough for the people at the counter to turn their heads. "That's the way with all you law types. Not worried about the facts, just about what happens in accordance with the law. Hardgrave was the same. Always concerned with the letter of the law."

"Judge Hardgrave?" The surprise was spread across Harvey's face.

"We were good friends. I hear that you knew him too, and I saw you at his funeral. He was a nice fellow. Old, but nice. A bit arrogant, but he had good connections."

"What was your relationship like with Hardgrave?"

"He helped me out when I needed it. And in turn,

I made sure that he had contact with his long-lost daughter, Michelle. Everyone was a winner in that relationship. It's amazing what an old man will do to try and erase past sins. You see, he treated Michelle like dirt while she was growing up. He never saw her, he beat her and her mother, he was a drunk; at least that's what Michelle has told me. But he wanted a second chance with her. He thought he deserved a second chance. And he was willing to do a lot to make sure that he got it."

"He would have hated you."

Lewis moved his hands to the table and gripped the edge until his knuckles turned white. "He liked me. And he loved his daughter."

It was clear that this man had anger management issues.

If anybody pushed the right buttons, Lewis wouldn't be able to hold back. His combination of arrogance, success, and testosterone had made him a melting pot of anger.

Not what Harvey needed right now.

"Hardgrave loved his daughter." Harvey lowered his tone of voice, trying to bring a sense of calm to the situation. "He would have done anything for her."

"He did like me." Lewis scoffed, defending his reputation. "He really liked my ties. I guess we could relate to each other in our shared ability to make the perfect color choice. He loved a well-tailored, brightly colored suit, as do I. I remember the last time we met, he said that my tie, this orange one that I'm wearing now actually, almost blended in exactly with his new armchair. He asked me to stand against it to check if the color matched, and sure enough, it did. We bonded over our love of color."

"It certainly is a brightly colored tie."

"It's my favorite. I have six ties the exact same as this one. Once I find something I really like, I try really hard to hold onto it. I even let Hardgrave borrow one of my ties once."

"Sounds like a charming little relationship."

"It certainly was as far as his daughter was concerned, too," Lewis quipped.

Harvey didn't answer; instead, he continued to stare at Lewis, watching how the man reacted under the silence. He sat comfortably, waiting for Harvey to continue. He was confident. Perhaps too confident. "Tell me about Detective Pitt."

"I don't have to tell you anything. If you want information, you can ask me nicely for it."

This was his turf. His place. And he was not going to spill the beans easily for a demanding lawyer.

Playing the game, Harvey retreated. "My apologies. For the sake of Carlos' freedom, can you please tell me what you know about Detective Pitt?"

"I know him." Lewis adjusted his tie so it pointed straight down the middle of his shirt. "Don't like him, though."

"Is he on the take?"

Lewis scrunched up his face a little, looking to the right and thinking hard. "Not that I know of. He could be, but I haven't heard it. Roberto knows him better than I do."

"Roberto Miles?"

"That's right. He and Pitt have had a few run-ins over the years. Pitt has arrested him a few times, but that was years ago. If someone arrested me, I would make sure that they paid the price for it, but not Roberto. Roberto seems to like talking to the

Smurfs."

The waitress' hand shook as she placed a coffee in front of Lewis, but he didn't even acknowledge her existence.

"Where were you and Carlos on the day that his house was raided?"

"At the diner. El Mejor. We went there a lot, and we had lunch, just the same as we had done many, many times before. Eating tacos and talking about the world. It was just another day for us. We're family. He's my cousin. We were just family talking about old times."

"No, you weren't."

The strong males locked eyes on each other, trying to assess who was more dominant.

"Did Carlos say that we weren't at the diner? I told him to stick by that story no matter what. I'm helping out my friend by saying that we were together." Lewis shook his head. "I would be surprised if Carlos said that we weren't at the diner. That would surprise me a lot."

"No, Carlos is sticking by the story that the two of you were at the El Mejor diner. It's the diner's surveillance footage that proves that you weren't there. There is no use bringing your lies to this table. I'm after the truth. That's the only thing that's going to help keep Carlos out of prison. The truth, Lewis."

"Surveillance footage? The diner has video cameras now?"

"Yes. And neither of you were there on September 12."

"Look." Lewis ran his fingers around the top of his mug of coffee. "Maybe we said the wrong diner. Maybe we were at another diner. Yeah, that's it. We were at another diner down the road. We felt like something different that day. It was another diner."

"One without video surveillance, I hope."

He nodded.

"The prosecution will ask you to testify that you were with Carlos that day."

"I won't go to court. Places like that are dangerous for men like me."

"They'll subpoena you to appear before the court. They want you on the stand, no matter what. And even if you change the story of your whereabouts on that day, they'll find another way to put you on the stand. You're their target, Lewis. They want you up there to be questioned under oath. They'll unload a barrage of questions, and you better bring your best game to the stand because they'll pounce on even the slightest mistake."

"I don't make mistakes."

"They'll pressure you until you crack. These people are the best in the game, and you're stepping into their ball court. They'll play you. My job is to make sure that my client isn't worse off because of your testimony."

"If they put me on the stand, then you can be guaranteed that I'll say anything that's in my best interest. Man, I'll even blame you for the drugs. I'll say anything. I'd be happy to lie in court."

"I'll pretend I didn't hear that."

"I don't care about your rules. I don't play your game. I make my living out here, in some of the most dangerous parts of the country. I'm not scared of an oath in court."

"If you make a mistake up there, then it'll be Carlos that pays the price. So where were you really on that day?"

"We were at a diner."

"I want the truth."

"You're not getting the truth. Not today, not ever. You will get whatever I decide to give you. And right now, I say that Carlos and I were in a diner together. You can choose which one. I don't care. You tell Carlos I said that, and I'm sure that he'll agree with me."

Harvey leaned forward on the table. "Let's get this straight, Lewis. I'm trying to keep your cousin out of prison. Don't let him go back there because of your pride. Help me out."

Lewis drew a long breath. Nothing meant more to him than family; his mother had taught him that.

"I don't like you." He paused and then exhaled. "But Carlos is family. Tell me what you need, and I'll make it happen."

"I need you to come into my office and go through your testimony. If your testimony fails to convince the court, then Carlos will go to prison. That's why I need you."

"I'm not going into your office," Lewis stated with disdain, but then he nodded, feeling defeated that he had no other choice but to help his cousin. "But send me a copy of your questions. I'll send you my answers, and you can tell me what else I need to say."

Lewis scribbled an email address on a napkin and tossed it in front of Harvey. He was not used to being defeated. Like a spoiled child, he always got his way.

"Let's work together to keep Carlos out of prison." Harvey threw a few dollars on the table and stood to leave.

Without taking his eyes off his coffee mug, Lewis

made sure he had the last word. "If you sell me out, I'll make sure that you pay the price. And it'll be a big price to pay."

CHAPTER 13

The phone vibrated in Harvey's pocket as he climbed into his car.

He'd expected as much. The purpose of the meeting with Juan Lewis was two-fold. One, to test the waters with a star witness, and two, to smoke out whether he was being followed.

It worked.

"Hello, Detective Pitt."

"That's quite formal for an old friend," Pitt stated. "Are you free for lunch?"

Harvey grinned to himself, making sure his smile wasn't big enough for his tail to see. "Yes, Pitt, I am."

Twenty minutes later, Harvey was sitting in another café just outside of USC. He sipped at the burnt coffee and ordered a serving of bacon and eggs, both of which he was sure would be burnt as well.

When Pitt arrived, he ordered the same before taking a seat opposite Harvey in the narrow booth. The vinyl seat stuck to his trousers as he struggled to get comfortable. From Harvey's lack of a greeting, he could tell that something was wrong.

Preemptively, Pitt struck first.

"Why did you need to meet with Lewis?"

"You tell me. You seem to know my movements quite well."

"I'm a cop. A detective," Pitt growled. "And Juan Lewis is a criminal. That's why I was tailing him. It's my job to catch criminals. And as a cop, I need to know why you met with Lewis."

"I'm a lawyer," Harvey retorted. "And it's my job to know things before the cops do."

His joke broke the tension. Pitt exhaled with a small laugh, leaning back in his chair as the waitress brought both their plates of overcooked scrambled eggs and burnt bacon to the table.

As the waitress walked away, Pitt commented, "Looks like they didn't burn it as much as last time."

Harvey shrugged. He much preferred his eggs overcooked and his bacon extra crispy. He liked the extra crunch.

"What did Lewis say?" Pitt wolfed down a fork full of scrambled eggs.

"Not a lot. I was touching base with a witness in my case." Harvey moved his bacon to the edge of the plate with his knife. "What did Roberto Miles say?"

Pitt shoveled in another mouthful of eggs. "Who?"

"Roberto Miles. It seems the two of you have a good relationship."

"Is that what Lewis said? Of course, he did. He would say that. He's just trying to cover his own butt, that's all. Misdirection. He's trying to make you think that Miles is the informer."

"Or you are."

Pitt put his fork down. "Harvey, you know me. You've known me for years. We're more than just colleagues trying to get justice. We're friends. You and me. You know I'm on the straight and narrow."

Whoever killed Hardgrave had no problem with knocking people off for self-preservation. Harvey needed to step carefully around Pitt or spend the rest of his days looking over his shoulder.

Taking out a criminal defense attorney would be child's play compared to killing a sitting judge.

"Of course." Harvey smiled, breaking the tension once more. "But it's always good to test the waters. Test your reaction."

"Ha! Still playing hypnotherapist, eh? You can't get that stuff out of your system. I'm sure that's why you're so good at what you do, Harvey."

In his previous career, Harvey had spent his time convincing people to break this addiction or that obsession. In hindsight, he understood that he was drawn to the profession because of his drug-addicted brother and found that helping others recover from their addiction felt like he was helping his brother.

And Pitt was right; sometimes, old habits were hard to break.

Harvey had spent his years as a lawyer not looking for mistakes in reports but looking for answers in the way a person's eyes moved, the way a person's head shook when they answered a question or the way a person's body betrayed what they were saying.

And that had won him a lot of cases.

"How's the Hardgrave case?"

"Not a lot of progress to report, I'm afraid. The killer was clean, left no evidence, and nobody's talking. Nobody saw anything, Harvey. But that's not uncommon in these parts. People don't like to talk to us or be seen talking to us. We expected that."

"Don't spin me that media line, Pitt. Save that for the press conferences. You must have something on somebody somewhere."

"I'm afraid not. I really wish I wasn't telling you

the truth, Harvey, but we have nothing. We've got six detectives working on this, and we have nothing."

"You're still the lead?"

"Of course. But these guys—they aren't pulling up the right information. They're missing something. A piece of the puzzle. But we'll find a suitable suspect and charge them. If nothing else, just to get the media off our back."

After only a few mouthfuls, Harvey pushed his plate slightly away, not comfortable in the present company anymore. He left a few bills on the table before choosing his next words very carefully.

"Something is wrong with this group of drug dealers," he said. "Someone is protecting them."

Pitt paused and looked straight up at Harvey. "If that's the case, you have to be careful who you talk to."

"I always am, Pitt."

But this time, he wasn't so sure.

CHAPTER 14

"These are dangerous men, Bill."

Jack Grayson's long limbs filled the front seat of Harvey's sedan, and his knees were squashed against the dash despite the leather seat being as far back as it could be.

Bill Harvey had spent extra on the latest model Mercedes-Benz S-class sedan for comfort, knowing he'd be conducting a lot of meetings there and that Jack needed the extra legroom. He was the same. His knees often hurt after long car journeys.

Parked next to Santa Monica beach, they conducted their meeting in the comfort of the air-conditioning, but with the added benefit of the iconic Californian view. Sun-drenched the sand before them, the heavy waves of the Pacific Ocean crashing on the shore. Despite the half-hour drive from his office, there was no use living in L.A. if you weren't going to take advantage of its many assets.

"How dangerous?" asked Harvey.

"I followed Roberto Miles yesterday afternoon—tailed him from when he left the house and saw him drive to an old estate. Three men went into a warehouse, and only two came out. That's how dangerous."

"Who was the third?"

"A low-level drug dealer who wasn't paying his debts. He won't be missed."

Harvey drew a long breath, looking out to the beach in front of them. Once, he dreamed of coming to L.A. and surfing each morning, working by day, and partying by night.

Traffic squashed that dream.

Reaching around to the back seat, he lifted up a box of doughnuts off the leather interior, offering Jack one first.

"Doughnuts?" Jack laughed. "Are you serious? Have you turned into a stereotypical stakeout cop now?"

"No." Harvey laughed with him. "I just had a craving for doughnuts this morning."

"I have never known you to eat doughnuts, Harvey. Usually, it's only carrot sticks and apples in your car, and you use whiskey as your only vice. Numbing your emotions with fatty food is something new."

"You know, maybe I should look for another vice. Maybe it's not all that healthy drowning my emotions in glasses of whiskey."

A moment of silence drifted over them… and then they both burst out laughing.

"Go on, give me one then." Jack laughed heartily. "I bet these are doughnuts baked with a whiskey glaze!"

"I wish." Harvey laughed with him.

They sat chuckling to themselves, each one biting into a plain glazed doughnut. They had never felt more like cops on a stakeout.

"What else have you got?"

"He's connected. Really well-connected." Jack

licked his fingers. "You know, we should eat doughnuts more often. That was delicious."

"It's not whiskey, but it's not bad." Harvey did the same. Index finger, middle finger. Right hand. Left hand. "But tell me more about Miles."

"He must be very well-connected because he seems to be a step ahead of everyone. After he walked out of the warehouse, the cops arrived only a few minutes later. He knew the cops were coming, and he knew when to bail out of there. Only someone who is very well-connected would know that."

"How many cops came to the warehouse?"

"I didn't stick around to find out. I heard the sirens coming and then got out of there myself. It wouldn't have looked too good if I was caught there."

"Understandable. Any idea who he's connected to?" Harvey asked the question, although he already knew the answer.

"Word on the street is that some detectives in the department want to make a bit of extra money on the side. Send their kids to a good college. You can't do that on a straight cop's wage."

"No names?"

"Not yet." Jack looked out the window as a girl in a bikini zipped past on rollerblades. "But I'll tell you something, Harvey. People are scared of these guys. These men take people out who get in their way. A lot of people, even my best informants, were reluctant to talk about Lewis or Miles. I didn't get a lot of information, but what I do know is that these men have killed before and wouldn't hesitate to do it again."

"I'm starting to get that impression."

"And if you think you're going to pin the Carlos

drug case on Lewis, then you better be prepared to be attacked. If anyone goes sniffing in their dirt, they usually end up missing. I was careful to cover my tracks, but they know you're defending Carlos. Word is, Miles is on high alert at the moment. A big drug run is coming up from Mexico shortly, and he's nervous about all the attention Carlos is getting."

"Was Hardgrave's name mentioned by anybody?"

"No. All I know is that they're connected to somebody."

"I heard that Hardgrave pointed Lewis in the direction of the cops, who could be bought with a few dollars. I think that's where they got their start."

"So Hardgrave was dirty?"

"No." Harvey eyed another doughnut. "He was desperate to see his daughter and the information he gave away seemed to be common knowledge anyway. I understand the desperation to see his only child."

"Do you know who they're connected to on the inside?"

"I tailed Miles two days ago and saw him talking to Pitt."

"Matthew Pitt?"

"That's right. They were talking quietly in a bar on Rodeo Drive. It was busy enough for them not to get seen together, but not quiet enough to raise suspicion. It was the perfect cover for an off-the-books chat."

"So he's dirty?"

"I don't know. I'm digging around to try and find that out."

"Be very careful where you dig. These men have no issue with violence."

"That's never stopped me before, Jack. Justice shouldn't run away from danger."

"But this is the next level, Harvey. I know you love danger, but this is different. This is like going on a theme park ride and not buckling up. You might get more of a rush, but you might also end up flying into the crowd below. Be careful."

Harvey looked out to admire the view again, studying the distant horizon. If this was to be one of his last days, then he wanted this to be one of his final memories—sitting in a car with his good friend, staring at the vast blue ocean.

A moment of real emotion that he didn't want to be drowned out by whiskey.

"I'm serious, Bill. Maybe you should leave the Hardgrave murder to the cops and just focus on your case. That case is taking you close enough to these guys. If they get wind that you're looking into the Hardgrave murder as well, then they'll come after you. Hard."

"Hardgrave was a good man, and he deserves justice. I can't trust the cops to deliver justice to the murderer."

"Just… be careful." There was a high level of fear in Jack's voice that Harvey hadn't heard before.

And that alarmed him.

A lot.

CHAPTER 15

Kate attacked her keyboard with intense vigor, punching in notes while they were fresh in her head. Her investigation skills weren't as polished as her boss's, but she thrived on the challenge. Being involved in the cases and being part of the action made her heart pump. It made her feel alive.

She barely stopped tapping the keyboard as Harvey strode back into his office.

"That must've been a long chat with Lewis," she said, not taking her eyes off the computer screen in front of her.

"It wasn't just coffee with Lewis; I stopped for a bite of lunch, and then a few doughnuts before I came back here. We don't have any meetings this afternoon, do we?"

"Nothing on the schedule, boss," she said, still not taking her eyes away from her work. "How was lunch?"

"Interesting," Harvey responded, standing in front of her desk. "I had lunch with a detective working the Hardgrave murder."

"Oh yes." Kate stopped typing and looked up at Harvey, fluttering her eyelids. "Anything that you wish to share?"

Average grades at school meant Kate never

expected to work in a job that she loved.

Not that she wasn't smart; she was just too busy boosting her self-esteem by chasing boys. After graduation, she expected that she would spend her life working in a call center, staring at a computer screen, keying personal details into a computer program, allowing the walls of boredom to slowly close in on her. When her first husband swept her off her feet with roses, flashy cars, and expensive restaurants, she thought she had been saved from a life of monotony.

Unfortunately, it was all a show. The man had a few dollars of inheritance, which he blew very quickly and then never worked a day in his life. He still hadn't.

The money caused her to overlook a lot of things, but when the glitz and glamour dried up, she was left with a deadbeat who would spend his days playing on his computer, drinking, and smoking. She struggled for years to recapture those fleeting few moments of young love before she kicked him out.

But he did give her the gift of a beautiful son, and for that, she was thankful, even if she had to support him by herself now.

When she first attempted to reenter the workforce as a fraught single mother, she never imagined that she would land a job that she loved.

"They don't have any public leads for the Hardgrave murder, and the pressure is mounting." Harvey picked up the postal mail on the edge of Kate's desk, scanning through the return addresses to determine their possible content. "And the media are getting desperate. They want a lead. They want something on this story. It's not a good look for the police department when they have a judge murdered in his own home, and they have no one to pin it on. The people want a suspect, and they haven't fronted one yet."

"So they have nothing? Not a thing?"

"They have everything they need. I'm just not sure they're doing what they need to do." He slowly opened a plain, white envelope with no return address. "They're currently looking at a few drug connections, which are also connected to our client."

"Lewis and Miles?"

"That's right. And it's obvious that they're tailing Lewis because as soon as I finished my coffee with him, they called me and offered to buy me lunch. That certainly wasn't a coincidence."

He opened the envelope and looked inside.

One photo, nothing more.

No letter. No note.

"Could you help them out with any information?" asked Kate.

"No. Lewis didn't give me a lot to go on. But I would bet that he's lied so many times that he wouldn't even know what the truth is anymore. He wouldn't even know how to tell the truth. What we do know is Lewis was dating Hardgrave's daughter. Lewis has an alibi for the time of Hardgrave's death, which coincidently is also the time my client's apartment was being raided."

"And Carlos is the alibi?"

"That's right. But I don't think they were really together at the time. They're both sticking to the story that they were at a diner having lunch, but it clearly isn't true."

"Did you tell the detectives that?"

Slowly, Harvey removed the photo from the envelope.

"I would never jeopardize my client's case. If it comes out in court that they weren't together, then that's another thing. Let's hope that the prosecution doesn't push that line of questioning too far because it wouldn't look good for Carlos if he's caught lying along with Lewis. They might as well call him guilty now if that happens."

"But you think one of them is involved in the Hardgrave murder?"

"I'm not sure…" Harvey's focus had turned to the letter.

He turned the photo over and stared at it—a color 4x6 inch photo of their office front door.

Slowly, he turned around and looked at the door. "When did this letter arrive?"

"Just this morning," Kate responded. "The letter came in with all the others. What is it?"

"A photo."

"Of?"

"Our office."

"And that's it? No other letter inside?"

He looked again inside the envelope. "Nothing."

"No return address?" Kate questioned.

He stared at the front door. "Kate, you need to take a few days off."

"No," she argued. "I want to come in. I want to help with these cases."

"No." He shook his head while the thoughts raced through it.

"I promise I'll be careful, Bill. I'll lock the doors and keep an eye out for anything unusual."

He stared at her, his eyes narrowing as he stared down at the person who knew him the best. "I'm not risking you for this case."

"Sorry, boss." She held his glare. "But that's not your choice."

CHAPTER 16

After checking the adjoining parking lot for any sign of activity, Harvey returned to his office, flipping through paperwork, ticking boxes, and signing his name where appropriate.

The photo was a clear threat.

He had dug too far into the world of the drug dealers, and now they knew about Kate. He couldn't risk her. His heart wouldn't take it.

When it was only his neck on the line, he was comfortable. If his time had come, then he could accept that. But when the threat came against one of the few people he really cared about, his attitude changed.

"Bill?" Kate entered his office quietly, a file against her chest. "I've been thinking about that photo."

"Go on."

"Maybe I dug a little too deep with Michelle—"

"No. Kate, this isn't about you. This isn't about what you've done. We're dealing with some very evil people, and they don't play nicely. It's nothing to do with you and everything to do with them. Don't blame yourself for this."

"Thanks, Bill." Kate gently sat down on a chair in the spacious, well-lit office. "We know why Lewis would want Hardgrave dead—"

"Why?" Harvey steered his attention away from

the paperwork.

"Because he's dating his daughter, and he's a big-name drug dealer. That lines up for me. Every judge in this country is concerned about his or her reputation, and having a daughter who's addicted to drugs is one thing… but having a daughter addicted to drugs and dating a drug baron is another thing altogether. I bet that Judge Hardgrave was pushing to have Lewis locked up, and Lewis wouldn't have liked that at all."

"Hardly a motive that would convict a man of murder."

"But it's a start. And look, I'm the secretary; you're the lawyer; if I come up with the theories, you can prove them." Kate smiled cheekily. "That's how teams work."

"We're a good team," Harvey agreed.

"I'll tell you something about Carlos," Kate stated firmly. "He looks off."

"Off?"

"Yeah, like something isn't right in his head. He looks like he could easily kill someone. He just has that look in his eyes, Bill. That creepy, faraway look. I have seen it before, and I know that working in this office, I'll see it again. He looks off."

"He might have been in the past, Kate," Harvey said, again in agreement. "He was heavily involved in the drug trade. That was his life, and I'm sure he's seen death many times before. But he changed. He went to prison, and he changed. He's been doing good recently, Kate. He's been helping drug addicts reform, and he's doing it all without a dollar of payment. That's not the behavior of a killer. That's a man who has recognized he has sinned and is trying to right the wrongs of his past. He's after redemption for the pain he caused."

"Maybe he's just doing the good deeds because of his guilt."

"Maybe. Regardless of the reason he's doing it, he's still doing good. He's still making a change in the world. And I truly think he wants to do good in this world and leave his mark. I think he wants to be remembered for making the world a better place, not for being a part of the drug trade. He's creating his legacy."

"You've been wrong before." Kate smiled, knowing that Harvey hated that line.

"Once," he stated firmly. "And you've never let me forget it. What have you found out about Michelle?"

Kate flipped open the file in her hands, reviewing the notes. "I did everything quietly, like you said. First, I did lots of online research, and I found her social media accounts, which included lots of photos. She has an account with all the big social media sites and makes a lot of comments on some blog posts."

"And?"

"Most of her photos on social media are of her alone—a lot of selfies. On her Facebook account, she posts lots of tough quotes, like this one: I don't need anybody. The strongest look after themselves. Or this one: Sometimes, it's better to be alone. Then nobody can hurt you. There were lots of quotes like this posted on her accounts."

"Sounds like somebody who has been hurt in the past."

"So, then I asked around a few dirty bars in East

L.A. that she had checked into on social media, and a few people knew her. I was told that she was a thief, a violent person, and a mean woman. She's not a nice girl, Bill. Nobody had anything nice to say about her. It's not a pretty picture at all. If she were a painting, she would be 'The Scream'—that's how bad I think she is."

"That's what happens when you spend a decade addicted to drugs. She's got a long record as well. Lots of pickups for drugs and petty theft. Lots of minor charges, some stints behind bars, but nothing major. Did you see her in person?"

"Only once. It was just a coincidence, and I didn't mean to see her, but I was in Walmart, and this skinny woman pushed past everyone in the line, swearing loudly and yelling that she needed a smoke. Nobody argued with her. I think everyone was scared of her. She even threatened to punch the attendant if she didn't hurry up."

"Not a pretty picture at all."

Kate picked up the L.A. Times from Harvey's desk and opened it to the social section. "I read this on the way in this morning. Her father got a good write-up in this article about social change. Apparently, before he died, he started a movement called 'Cake with a Friend.' It was to combat loneliness in the older generation. They must have thought he was very special because there's even a color photo of him. Here, he's reading calmly in his living room. I want to look that calm when I'm seventy years old."

She handed the paper across to Harvey, and he rustled through the pages. "That's a nice photo of Hardgrave. He looks very comfortable in his old age. Calm. Relaxed. Happy."

"Crazy living room, though," Kate commented on the picture.

"He was always known for being very eccentric. I remember five years ago, he bought a brand-new Aston Martin that was gray in color. Everyone was surprised that he would buy such a plain-looking car. One week later, he comes back with the car, and he has had it spray-painted bright yellow. The yellowest car I have ever seen. It looked like a long banana."

Kate smiled at the thought. "But who has a purple armchair in their living room? That's not eccentric—that's just bad taste."

"Purple armchair?"

"That's right. Look at the color of his armchair in the picture. It's purple. That's crazy. It says in the article that he was known for his choice of bright colors all throughout his house."

"But the chair in the living room is purple…"

"So?"

"Hardgrave was shot on an orange armchair. The crime scene pictures made the blood spatter look like a Jackson Pollock painting. Kate, get me the timeframe of the delivery of the new armchair to Hardgrave's house."

"Why? What does that mean?"

Harvey didn't respond.

Instead, he leaned back in his chair, a grin on his face.

CHAPTER 17

The sweat started to dampen his armpits. Harvey's fists were held tightly. His jaw was clenched. This was the moment he loved. This was the moment he lived for.

The courtroom was alive with energy, anticipation, and apprehension.

The room was well-lit, the pews behind them filled with onlookers, and the tension in the air was palpable. The court clerk stood steady at the head of the room, awaiting the arrival of the judge and jurors, the people who would help decide the fate of Carlos López.

Harvey drew a deep breath, glancing over to the prosecution's table led by Miss Shannon Chettle. She was busily tidying her desk, distracting herself from the anxiety. She moved a pen holder to the right, the laptop slightly to the left, and rearranged the files on her desk in order. When she caught Harvey grinning at her, she almost cut through him with a death stare.

He understood her nerves. Not many jobs captured this much public attention. One small slip of the tongue and you could find yourself leading the news bulletins. One wrong sentence, and all of a sudden, your name is mud.

That's pressure.

"Two minutes," the court clerk called out, alerting them to the fact that the spectacle was about to begin.

This was it.

His moment.

He had the fate of Carlos López resting in his hands, and if he played his cards well, then the destiny of his client would be changed forever.

"All rise for the honorable Judge Windsor."

The tall, strong, and dominant figure of Judge Windsor slowly entered the room. He moved with strength, authority, and self-control. He was respected in the legal community as a hard but fair man.

After Judge Windsor had said his opening remarks, he welcomed the jury to the courtroom. Uneasily, they walked to their seats, a few bumping their legs along the way. They knew that, at this point, the eyes of the court were on them. For anyone not used to public performance, that burden could almost melt them into a puddle.

The jurors appeared to be a good group—a solid bunch of working-class citizens. Just what Harvey wanted. He made sure that there were no millionaires, no Hollywood wannabes, and no Beverly Hills snobs in that box. He wanted twelve people who could relate to his client and understand the struggles of a man living in East L.A. He used every objection he had and ended up with the people he wanted.

Surprisingly, the prosecution didn't dismiss the two jurors with Mexican heritage. Harvey was sure that Chettle would use her objections to knock those two out.

But she didn't.

And for the life of him, Harvey couldn't

understand why.

Based on the way the jurors with Mexican heritage were assessing Carlos, he could tell that they had already identified with his client. If one of them refused to find Carlos guilty based on their similar upbringings, then he had already won the case. If one person held true in that jury room, for whatever reason, then the case was a mistrial. The prosecution had the option of bringing another case against him, but unless they had new evidence, that was unlikely. All he needed was that one person on the jury, and he already knew his targets.

Carlos López sat next to Harvey as a well-dressed, respectable member of the community. A man whose face showed that he had done his time but who now knew the value of helping others. That's what Harvey would play up. There was no logical reason why a man who spent his spare time helping others overcome drug addiction would still be dealing drugs.

Harvey only had to create reasonable doubt for Carlos to walk away, and based on the lack of substantial evidence, he was sure that he could do that. Words were his weapon, and he was ready with the heavy artillery.

His main threat was the way that Chettle would spin the case. She would go big on the evidence and thick on the facts. They would be repeated time and time and time again in this case.

The true facts of the case were indisputable. A briefcase full of drugs was found in the apartment belonging to Carlos López. That was fact.

But there was no one home when the LAPD raid happened—and that left enough room for Harvey to create reasonable doubt about who the briefcase belonged to.

With two days scheduled for the prosecution's case and one day for the defense's case, the court was expecting a quick turnaround. They had other cases to get to, bigger, more high-profile than just another drug possession charge.

The prosecution was clearly disappointed that Carlos didn't take the deal to roll over on Lewis. After the failed raid, that was the angle they were hoping for. But when Carlos refused to turn over on his family, they had to press ahead with the charges, or they would appear powerless.

All the hollow threats they'd made trying to convince Carlos to roll over on his cousin would be remembered by the criminal community for a long time. No one would be threatened by a prosecution that couldn't convict a common drug dealer.

After Judge Windsor had talked to the jurors, Chettle was ready to lay all her cards out on the table. This was the moment Harvey had been waiting for—what does she have up her sleeve? How will she approach the weak case that she couldn't afford to lose?

Chettle opened her statement sitting behind her desk, but when she got into her speech, she stood and slowly moved around the table.

Harvey liked the way she moved. Her hips had a gentle swing to them.

"On September 12 of this year, the Los Angeles

Police Department raided the home of Carlos Maxwell López. They made this raid based on intelligence gathered from a source close to Mr. López. After they entered the apartment, they found $50,000 worth of heroin in a briefcase located in Mr. López's bedroom, next to his bed.

$50,000 worth of heroin.

Those are the facts. Plain and simple.

Plain and simple.

I will repeat them for you—$50,000 worth of heroin in Mr. López's bedroom, next to his bed.

That is fact.

There is no doubt about that.

Over the coming days, you will be presented with those facts as the core of this case. That's the reason we're here today. That's why you're sitting in this courtroom.

The average person does not have $50,000 worth of heroin lying around their apartment. No. This is no accident. This is not a chance encounter. It was not some strange coincidence.

Carlos López owned those drugs.

$50,000 worth of heroin.

It was enough to destroy lives, and it was enough to destroy families.

We need these drugs off the streets. And we need men like Carlos López off the streets as well.

Now, the defense might argue about the reason the briefcase was in his apartment. They might even say that he didn't own the briefcase, but that's not going to work this week. Not here. Not in a place where we make judgments on the facts.

It won't work because I trust you.

I trust that you will make a decision based on the

facts of this case.

And the facts are plain and simple.

There is no arguing against the facts.

In Carlos López's apartment, where he lives alone, a briefcase full of heroin was found. Those are the facts, ladies and gentlemen.

The facts.

Cold, hard facts.

Nobody else lives with Mr. López. Nobody else was in his apartment when it was raided. Those are facts.

The facts.

The drugs were in his possession.

In law, we have a term called 'constructive possession of illegal narcotics.' Constructive possession is when drugs clearly belong to a person; however, the person wasn't carrying the drugs at the time. For a court to determine constructive possession, it's very simple. There must be two key elements: one; the defendant must have knowledge of the location of the drugs, and two; the defendant must have the ability to exercise authority and control of the drugs.

It's very simple.

Carlos López had knowledge of the drugs' whereabouts—they were in his apartment. In his bedroom. Next to his bed. Undoubtedly, he knew they were there. Undoubtedly, they were his.

Carlos López had the ability to exercise control of these drugs. Nobody else did. Nobody else had a key to his apartment. Carlos López stated that fact in a sworn police statement. He's the only person who was able to exercise control of his apartment and its contents. Among those contents was the briefcase full of drugs.

I will repeat: the drugs were in his possession.

It is that simple.

My name is Shannon Chettle, and with my team, we will present evidence that will leave you with no choice but to convict Mr. López. You will have no choice because he's guilty.

He owned the briefcase full of drugs. They were in his possession.

Without the interference of the hardworking police officers, those drugs would have ended up on the streets. Without the interference of the police raid, those drugs would have made it out into the hands of the people of Los Angeles. Out onto the street, where they would attack vulnerable people. Jeopardizing the lives of the defenseless people of this country.

That's what drugs do—they attack the weak.

We must stop the suppliers. We must stop people like Carlos López from bringing more drugs onto the streets. If we don't stop him today, then I can guarantee you he'll do it again. He'll find more drugs. More briefcases.

That's how the cycle works.

This week, you have an opportunity to make our city safer. Cleaner. You have the chance to save lives.

Over the coming days, we will present witnesses to you who will explain this case in more detail. LAPD Detectives will tell you why they chose to raid Carlos López's apartment on September 12. Police officers will detail how the raid unfolded. Forensic experts will explain what they found in the apartment. We will hear from witnesses who will testify about Carlos López's whereabouts on that day.

You will be presented with a lot of information over the coming days, but you must focus on one thing—the evidence. That's what you have to focus on in this case.

And if you look at the evidence, if you look only at the proof, then it will lead you to only one possible conclusion—the briefcase full of drugs could only be deemed to be in possession of Carlos López.

He must be found guilty of this crime.

Your job on the jury is clear—you will listen to the evidence and make a determination on that evidence. Once you have seen the evidence, your decision will be easy.

At the end of this case, I will not stand before you and give you an answer. I already know the answer based on the evidence.

But it's not for me to decide.

No.

It's for you to make a decision based on all the evidence presented to you.

That's all I ask you to do.

It will be clear. Your only possible choice will be to find Carlos López guilty of the charges of felony drug possession.

Thank you for serving your duty to this great city."

Bill Harvey glanced at Chettle as she walked back to her table. He appreciated her great performance. He almost felt that he should stand and clap as she sat down.

After only one speech, Chettle already had the jury

in her capable hands. They already wanted to believe her every word. Her voice was so soft and sensual that it could melt even the harshest person.

"May it please the court, Miss Chettle, members of the jury, on September 12, a briefcase full of drugs was found in an apartment in East L.A. As the prosecution had informed you, your job as a member of this jury is to reach a verdict based on the evidence that is presented to you.

Not assumptions—but the evidence.

Now let me explain the difference to you:

Evidence is defined as the available body of facts indicating whether a belief is true or valid. That is evidence.

An assumption is defined as a thing that is accepted without proof.

There is no evidence that proves the briefcase containing drugs belonged to Mr. Carlos López. There are no fingerprints on the briefcase, no DNA, and no video footage of Mr. López with the briefcase. There is no evidence of Mr. López carrying the briefcase, and there is no evidence to confirm that he was even near the briefcase at any time.

No evidence.

In this court of law, you cannot convict a man if you have reasonable doubt about the accusations. What is reasonable doubt? It's doubt that still exists upon reason and common sense after a careful and impartial consideration of the evidence.

My name is Bill Harvey, a criminal defense attorney, and along with my team, I represent Mr. Carlos López. I am here to explain to you the undeniable fact that right now, Carlos López is presumed innocent.

My team and I are here to help you understand the many reasonable doubts that lurk in the assumptions brought before you by the prosecution. And they're just that—assumptions, not evidence.

This trial will be an interesting journey, but it's one that we will take together.

I will help you on this journey, and I will present evidence to you, beginning with my cross-examination of the prosecution's evidence. I will show you where the reasonable doubt lies. Together, you and I will work as a team to show the prosecution that they have made a mistake.

People make mistakes, even police officers.

That's why we have a court system. That's why police officers don't decide the guilt or innocence of the people they arrest.

We will present witnesses who will testify about Carlos López's long history of volunteering. They'll testify that Carlos López spends his time helping others overcome drug addictions. That's right. This man is against drugs. Against drugs. He dedicated his life to helping people recover from drug addictions; he didn't put them there. He even had a room in The East Rehabilitation Center named after him. That's how much he cares about helping people.

He wants to save people from addiction, not encourage it.

I will help you, and together, we will find Carlos López 'Not Guilty' based on the reasonable doubt that lies within the prosecution's assumptions.

You will have reasonable doubt at the end of this case. And you cannot convict a man based on assumptions.

Thank you for your time, and thank you for listening."

CHAPTER 18

For LAPD Detective Roger Townsend, there was no gray in life. Everything was black and white, including his clothes.

He wasn't interested in the rule of law as it was written by the politicians; his rules were governed by his moral compass, created during a hard childhood with a very religious family. He was as uncompromising in his police work as he was rigid in his Christian faith. It took him many years to earn a seat in the front pew of the church, and he would never let it go. He stood there every Sunday morning with his devout family, singing heartily at every hymn, brashly reciting every prayer, taking his faith very seriously.

As the lead detective in the raid that led to the drug bust, Townsend came to the stand as the prosecution's first witness.

Bill Harvey and Roger Townsend had clashed over a drug case before, and Harvey was certain that the evidence had been planted at the scene of the crime.

Some criminals were impossible to catch even though everyone knew they were guilty. The people on the street knew it, the cops knew it, and even the shopkeepers knew it. But they had to be caught in the act. In their last case, Townsend had planted the evidence in the car of a suspect, one small bag of cocaine, just to take a criminal off the street. They'd struck a favorable deal for the client, mostly because the prosecution didn't want the evidence tested in a court of law.

And Harvey was comfortable with that process. Just because the police couldn't catch someone didn't mean they weren't guilty.

After the ink was dry on the deal, Townsend took Harvey aside. "If a heroin deal happens and there are no police there to witness it, is it still a crime?" he grumbled. "Of course it is. A crime is a crime regardless of the evidence gathered. A criminal is a criminal regardless of when, or how, they're caught."

Although he didn't want to, Harvey had to agree. That statement made perfect sense outside the walls of the courthouse.

But inside the courthouse was a different scenario.

Inside these walls, evidence mattered, not a moral compass.

The issue for Harvey was that the police weren't even after his client when they conducted the raid. They didn't want to arrest Carlos. They didn't want to put him behind bars. They wanted to sacrifice an innocent man in the hope that it put pressure on the kingpin.

That was not acceptable.

As Juan Lewis had no previous criminal convictions, the LAPD Gang and Narcotic Division Detectives weren't able to gather enough evidence to be approved for a warrant to search his premises. However, Carlos López, with his previous conviction, became their easy target. They expected Lewis to be in the apartment when they conducted the raid. When they found that he wasn't there, they had to put the squeeze on Carlos until he gave up Lewis.

But Lewis and López were family, and Carlos wasn't going to sell his cousin out, especially not to the police.

The defense attorney believed that Carlos was speaking the truth when he said that the drugs weren't his. Every time Harvey asked the question, there was no hesitation, no attempt to disguise the truth. Carlos was firm and open.

The truth, however, wasn't part of his job.

His job was to defend his clients against the process of the judicial system. It was not up to him to make a determination of their guilt.

Detective Townsend sat on the witness stand wearing an old black and white suit, perhaps the same suit he wore to his wedding twenty years ago. His smile was self-righteous, his superiority was strong, and his tolerance was low.

Despite his great respect for the people who serve his community, Harvey had little respect for Townsend as a person. He understood that Townsend risked his life every week for the safety of the public and, for that, he was indebted; however, that didn't make his personality likable.

If Townsend hadn't been a detective, Harvey would have knocked his teeth out a long time ago.

"Please state your name and occupation for the purposes of the court."

"Detective Roger Denis Townsend. I have been a proud member of the LAPD for thirty years. I have seen a lot in that time."

"I bet you have," Chettle stated almost flippantly. Her personal dislike for Townsend was also clear. His old-school behavior, mostly bordering on sexual harassment, didn't sit well with this feminist. "Did you apply for a search warrant for the apartment belonging to Juan Lewis but rented by Carlos López?"

"That's correct."

"Is this the search warrant?" Chettle presented the warrant to the witness.

"It is."

"Is there anything wrong with this warrant? Anything unlawful?"

"It's a valid and lawful search warrant."

"Thank you, detective," she continued. "Please explain to the court what happened after you received the warrant to search Carlos López's apartment on September 12."

"After the warrant was granted to enter Carlos López's apartment, we scoped out the premises for two hours. I was positioned across the street with Detective Bloom in our sedan while another two detectives watched the back door of the apartment complex to ensure that nobody used that as an exit." Detective Townsend's voice was rough and harsh.

"And did anybody enter the apartment during that time?"

"Yes. We saw Carlos López and Juan Lewis enter the apartment building at approximately 10:14 am."

"Can you please explain to the court who Juan Lewis is?"

"He's the owner of the apartment that Carlos López was renting. He's also a cousin of Carlos López."

"Were either of them carrying anything?"

Townsend leaned back in the stand, straightened

his shoulders, and flattened the tie down the middle of his shirt. "We saw Carlos López carrying a black briefcase."

With his small grooming activities, Townsend was dispersing nervous energy. That small movement might be overlooked as normal by the casual observer, but not by Bill Harvey.

"Did you see either of them leave the apartment building?"

"No. We had detectives positioned at the back door of the building, and they didn't see them leave the building."

"And you believed that Carlos López and Juan Lewis were in the apartment at the time of the raid?" Chettle continued.

"We did."

Carlos leaned forward, twitching his leg nervously under the table.

"How long was the time between when you saw Mr. Lewis and Mr. López enter the apartment, with Mr. López carrying the briefcase, and when you decided to enter the apartment with the search warrant?"

"Around thirty minutes."

"And why was there a delay?"

"We had to wait for the uniformed police officers to arrive to assist with the search. We were watching the apartment, so we were confident that Lewis and López were still in the apartment at the time we conducted the raid."

"But they weren't, were they?"

"No, they weren't."

"If you had detectives at the back door to the apartment building, and you were watching the front of the building, where were they?"

"We later found a third exit to the building—an old, barely used window in the laundry room on the east side of the building. This window led to the parking lot next door. Lewis and López must have left the building via this exit."

"Why would they have done that?"

"I imagine that this was an attempt to avoid—"

"Objection," Harvey stated, not looking up from his notepad. "Not factual."

"Sustained," Judge Windsor replied. "Please stick to the facts as you know them, Detective Townsend."

"Yes, Your Honor." Townsend nodded like a little schoolboy after he had been told off by the headmaster. "In my professional opinion, I would suggest…" He paused and waited for the objection, but when none was forthcoming, he continued, "I would suggest that they were trying to avoid detection; otherwise, they would have left via one of the main exits."

"Please, detective, take us through what happened after you made the decision to enter the apartment building."

"Once the uniform backup arrived, another four officers, we made the decision to enter the apartment building. As is normal procedure, we went to the apartment door, apartment 214 on the second floor, identified ourselves, and waited for an answer. And when we didn't receive an answer, we entered the apartment, again identifying ourselves as LAPD police officers."

"Did anybody answer once you identified yourselves?"

"No."

"And did you use force to enter the apartment?"

"Yes, we did. When there was no answer, we breached the door using a battering ram. That's normal procedure for a raid."

"And once you entered the apartment that belonged to Juan Lewis and was rented by Carlos López, what did you find?"

"Nothing unusual to start off with. We called out as we entered. Nobody responded. We cleared the premises to ensure that nobody was present, and that's when we began the search."

"Were you surprised to find nobody at the premises?"

"Yes, we were."

Chettle paused for a few long moments, letting that fact sink into the minds of the jurors.

"Is this a layout of the premises?" Chettle presented a diagram to the court.

"It is."

"And are these the photos of the rooms that you took before you began the search?"

"They are." Townsend leaned to the left in his chair. "As a team, we searched the kitchen first, and then we each entered one of the other rooms to search on our own. I entered the main bedroom, and that's where I found the briefcase."

"Did you open the briefcase?"

"Yes. We believed there were drugs present on the property, and we knew we were going to have to perform a thorough search to find them. I thought the briefcase seemed like an obvious way to carry concealed drugs, and that's why I opened it. I placed the briefcase on the bed and popped open the locks. Inside, I found numerous plastic bags of white powder. This white powder later proved to be heroin, and the street value of the heroin was deemed to be $50,000."

"And this is the briefcase that you found?" Chettle introduced the briefcase as evidence, presenting it to the jury and the court.

It was cheap, black, and uncomplicated. The sort of briefcase a detective would buy from Walmart.

"That's the briefcase, yes."

"Is it normal for drugs to be transported via this type of briefcase?"

"It's not unusual, but drugs can be transported in anything. Bags, cars, clothes, postal service envelopes—you can find them stored anywhere. And that means we have to look everywhere. I could spend a whole day telling you about the strange places we have found drugs. So, no, the briefcase certainly wasn't an unusual place to find drugs."

"When did Carlos López return to the apartment?"

"He returned to the apartment just before 3:00 pm in the afternoon."

"And when he returned, what did you do?"

"We arrested Carlos López for the possession of drugs."

"Did you read him his Miranda rights after you made the arrest?"

"That's correct."

"Thank you, detective. No further questions."

"Defense, your witness," Judge Windsor called firmly.

Testing Townsend's patience, Harvey took time to review his notes. It was a deliberate ploy; he was asserting a sense of authority in the courtroom. This was his place, and now Townsend could play by his rules.

"Thank you for your time, Detective Townsend," he began after two long minutes of silence. "Did you take video evidence of the raid?"

"That's correct."

"And is this the video?" Harvey introduced the video to the court, pointing at the television screen at the side of the room.

"Yes, it appears so."

For the next six minutes, the court watched the beginning of the raid. Townsend called out for any persons present, broke through the door, ensured there were no other people in the apartment, and then began to conduct the search, leaving the small camera device resting on the kitchen counter.

"It's normal procedure to video a drug raid?" Harvey asked as he paused the recording.

"Where we have the resources to do it, we conduct raids using video recording."

"Why did you remove the video recording device from your shoulder and leave it on the kitchen counter?"

"When the premises had been secured, it's normal procedure to leave the recording device in a place that covers the greatest area for recording. In this case, it was the kitchen counter. You could see the hallway, part of the kitchen, and the living room."

"Is this you in the video?" The video paused at the moment when Townsend was walking down the hallway of the apartment.

"It appears to be me."

"And are you carrying a large gym bag as you walk down the hallway—before you enter the bedroom?"

"Ah." Townsend didn't expect that question. He thought he kept that bag out of view. "Yes. In that bag is the equipment that I needed to conduct the search."

"Such as?"

"Things needed to check the apartment."

"Is that bag large enough to fit a briefcase in it?"

"Objection!" Chettle called out. "What the defense is suggesting here has no evidence."

"Do you have any evidence that may support making that claim, Mr. Harvey?" Judge Windsor leaned forward and asked.

"No, Your Honor."

"Then the objection is sustained. Strike that question from the record. Move on, Mr. Harvey."

Chettle marked it down as a win for her, but the damage was already done—the jurors were already questioning whether the bag was large enough to have held the briefcase.

"And you entered the apartment with this bag? Is it usual procedure to enter an apartment with that bag at the time of a raid?"

"Listen." Townsend paused for a few moments. "It's not the usual procedure, and it's what I needed for that day."

"And this is the usual procedure, right?"

"No, but it's not unusual."

"Hmm…" Harvey paused again, not because he needed the time to think but because he wanted to give the jury a few moments to process the information. "Was anyone else in the bedroom when you found the briefcase?"

"No, not when I found the briefcase."

"Just you and this bag?"

Townsend hesitated before answering. "Yes."

"And, of course, you left the video camera in the kitchen, so there's no video of you in the bedroom before you opened the briefcase?"

"Before video recording, it was normal procedure to search a room without someone recording everything." His sarcasm was clear.

"You found the drugs when you were in the room by yourself, with the bag?"

"Yes." Townsend glared hard at the defense table.

"Nobody else saw the briefcase before you opened it?"

"That's correct."

"Just you?"

"Objection," Chettle called out. "Asked and answered. The witness has clearly answered this question already."

"Withdrawn." Harvey looked back down at his notes. "And tell me, who made the tip-off that there were drugs in the apartment?"

"It was an anonymous tip. It came through on our tip line."

"And is it usual procedure to raid every house mentioned in a tip via a telephone line?"

"No, but this tip gave quite detailed information about the drugs and their whereabouts, and given the criminal history of the resident, we made a decision to follow up on the tip-off. It proved correct."

"Did the tip provide details of who owned the drugs?"

"No, it didn't. It stated that the drugs would be at that location during that time. That's all we knew."

"Detective Townsend, did you make the arrest of Carlos López?"

"Yes." He rolled his eyes.

"Did you read him his Miranda rights when you arrested him?"

"Yes."

"And did he say anything when you arrested him?"

"He did."

"And what did he say?"

"He was innocent."

"Anything else?"

"Yes."

"And what was that?"

Townsend paused and sighed, adjusting his tie again. "He said that it was a setup. He said that the briefcase didn't belong to him."

"And who did he claim the bag belonged to?"

Townsend stared at Harvey and drew a long breath. "He claimed that the police planted the bag."

"Did he? Why would he say that?"

"Most criminals say that. It's their first reaction. They claim they have been set up and they don't own the goods. It's not true, though."

"Did Carlos López say that he didn't own the drugs and it was a setup?"

"Yes."

"And he stated that the police planted the bag?"

"That's what he stated."

"That's very interesting, Detective Townsend." Harvey wrote notes on his pad, prompting two of the jurors to do the same. "No further questions."

CHAPTER 19

For the rest of the afternoon, like a tedious fashion show for the courtroom, Chettle paraded the other cops who were present during the raid. She asked the same questions, time and time again, solidifying the facts in the jurors' minds.

By the time Judge Windsor had called an end to day one of the trial, most of the jurors felt like they'd been present at the time of the raid. They knew more about the raid than they did their own children.

After the jurors filed out of the courtroom, Chettle let her guard down and smiled. She was winning. She knew that. And what a win it would be—to take on the formidable Bill Harvey and walk away with success in court. She would be celebrated in the District Attorney's office like a hunter returning with a winter's kill. Her win would show them all that he was beatable.

But she knew that she shouldn't be celebrating yet. This was Bill Harvey, after all.

Glancing across at his desk, she noticed that he wasn't packing up. He wasn't making notes. He wasn't even talking to his client.

Bill Harvey was sitting stoically, pen in hand, staring into nothingness.

"Given up, Bill?" Chettle remarked.

The question snapped him out of his thoughts.

"No." He smiled. "Quite the contrary. I'm working hard."

"I'm not sure your client would agree." She gestured towards a nervous Carlos López talking to his supporters in the courtroom seats behind them. "It certainly doesn't look like you're working hard."

"Not all work happens on a piece of paper. Not all work can be defined in a new document."

"Most of it can," she retorted as she placed another heavy file in her bag.

"Once, a writer used to sit at his desk every day and stare out the window. His wife would walk past every morning and say the same thing, 'Not working today?' And he would always reply, 'I am. I'm doing the most important work there is.'"

Chettle shook her head, slightly confused. "And what was the most important work there is?"

"Thinking." Harvey smiled. "Nothing is more important than taking some time out to think."

"You're lucky you have the time to do that. I don't have the capacity to take some time out to think. I've got too much to do. I have to think on my feet."

"And that's why you'll lose this case."

Chettle stopped.

His confidence struck fear in her heart. Only moments earlier, she'd felt like she was going to be popping open the champagne bottles soon, but suddenly, she felt like she was being beaten.

She didn't say another word to Harvey; instead, she snapped at her team to pack up quickly and follow her out the door.

"Bill, how'd we do?" Carlos questioned once the prosecution team had exited the courtroom. His supporters weren't far behind them, but he had stayed to talk about the next steps with the head of his defense. "I thought you did well out there, and I can tell that juror of Mexican descent isn't going to say I'm guilty. There's something in his eyes that says that he has my back. The man that was sitting on the back left of the jury box is proud of his heritage. I can sense these things."

"We're doing okay." Harvey's answer was cold as he tidied his desk.

"But what does that mean? Are we in front?" Carlos tugged on Harvey's arm.

Harvey turned slowly and looked at Carlos. "Carlos, I don't think that today is going to matter much."

"I don't understand, Bill. You're going to have to spell it out for me." His voice was frantic. "All this courtroom stuff is over my head. It's all about the law, not about whether I'm actually innocent. You people are more worried about the way something is written in a book than whether or not that briefcase was mine."

"When we return to the courtroom tomorrow, we're going to make a play," Harvey stated slowly. "That play is going to change the entire course of this trial. If it works, nobody will remember what happened today."

"And if it doesn't work?"

"Then I hope you're right about your Mexican friend sitting in the jury box."

"That doesn't fill me with confidence, Bill." Carlos looked at the table in front of him. "I don't want to go back to prison. That's not where I belong."

"Carlos—"

"I help people out here. It's my life's purpose. I can make a difference in many people's lives. I can save people. But in prison, back behind bars, I'm just another drug dealer, and I don't know if I can make it through prison this time. I only just barely made it out with my life last time."

Harvey nodded. "Then let's hope our play works."

"What are you going to do?"

"You should focus on getting some rest." Harvey sighed. "I've got work to do to prepare for tomorrow."

Harvey looked down at his notes and studied them for a while before closing his briefcase. Carlos didn't leave. He couldn't. He needed more information.

"Where are you going?" The fear in Carlos' eyes was clear.

"I'm going to have a talk with Mr. Roberto Miles."

"Miles? No. You can't do that. That's too dangerous. You shouldn't talk to him. Lewis didn't appreciate your chat, and Miles will like it even less. Leave him alone; he's got nothing to do with this case."

"We need him in court."

"What for?"

"For the play that I'm talking about."

"I really don't understand. Why would you need Miles? He has nothing to do with this case."

"Lewis is due on the stand tomorrow, Carlos. The prosecution has subpoenaed him to testify that the two of you were together at the time of the raid. I think that's what they want. They want him on the stand to send a message that they're after him, and they're getting closer by the minute. They want him to make statements under oath. That's going to be our opportunity to blow this case wide open."

"So why do you need Miles?"

"Because they're all connected."

"He's dangerous. He's not the man you want to cross. He's not the type of man you want to make mad."

"Nor am I, Carlos."

CHAPTER 20

"Mr. Roberto Miles." Bill Harvey held out his weathered hand as a welcoming greeting.

Roberto Miles stared down at the hand, slowly raising his eyes to meet Harvey's. "And who are you?"

"I'm criminal defense attorney, Bill Harvey. I'm representing Carlos López in the current drug trial."

"The drugs weren't his. The cops planted it."

"I've heard that."

Roberto Miles stood eye to eye with Bill Harvey, two tall men standing on the steps of a pleasant house in Montebello, ten miles east of Downtown L.A. If it weren't for the two Bentleys, the Dodge Challenger and the Chevy Impala, parked on the lawn, this house could be mistaken for a picture of suburban middle-class bliss.

That, and the strong smell of marijuana pouring out the front door.

"What are you doing here? Shouldn't you be writing reports about how the police planted drugs at my friend's apartment? Isn't that what you lawyers do? Or are they paying you off as well?"

"My job isn't to write reports about the police on the take. My job is to investigate. And my investigations have led me here."

Roberto Miles stood on his front step, thinking so

hard that Harvey could almost see the thoughts clunk through his head. Dressed in a short-sleeved black shirt with the buttons done all the way to the top, Roberto didn't look like he was going to the opera. With the smell of marijuana almost soaked into his clothes, it was clear how Roberto was planning to spend the rest of his evening.

A mix of 1960s American and classic Mexican styling, the large two-story house sat on top of a hill at the end of a dead-end street, the perfect place to watch for any approaching cars. The garden was once a flowering maze of shrubs and bushes, but without the diligent care of the previous owners, the greenery had struggled to survive under the blaze of the Californian sun.

The current owners had been much too busy growing other plants.

"Are you a cop?"

"No. Like I said, I'm a lawyer, and I'm Carlos's lawyer. I'm on his side. I'm trying to get him off the drug possession charges, but to do that, I need your help. I need to talk to you about his case."

"You're on his side?" he confirmed.

"Yes."

Slowly, the thoughts continued to thump through his head, and eventually, he smiled. "Why didn't you say so? Any brother of Carlos' is a brother of mine!"

Roberto placed his arm around Harvey's shoulders, leading him into the dark house. Despite the sun just setting on the horizon, the blinds were drawn closed, and from the damp smell, it seemed like the inside of this house hadn't seen a touch of daylight in months.

Harvey was guided into the living room, where

two men were fixated on the flickering television in front of them, computer game controls being punched in their hands.

"No!" screamed one man. He stood up from the sofa, throwing the controller down in disgust. "I was duped, man. That should've been a foul! I should've been going to the free-throw line. You cheated, man!"

The other man on the couch giggled like a little schoolboy, dazed under the effects of smoking too much greenery.

"What's he doing here?" a shrouded man in the corner of the room, sitting by himself in an old armchair, called out.

"This is Bill Harvey, a friend of Carlos's." Miles patted his hand solidly on Harvey's back. "You know him?"

"Yeah, I know him, and I don't trust him."

Miles' hand reached for his right hip, where he was carrying a weapon under his shirt.

Harvey held up his hands in surrender. "Juan Lewis, it's good to see you again. I'm just here trying to get information to help Carlos get off these charges. Nothing sinister. I'm here trying to help Carlos. That's all."

Two of Miles' well-built friends stepped in from the next room as soon as they heard raised voices.

"Are we good?" Miles asked Lewis, his hand still on his right hip.

"Whatever." Lewis shrugged. "Let him in. The guy's harmless."

"He doesn't look harmless," Miles commented, looking Harvey up and down. "He looks like he can handle himself. So, are we good?"

"Yeah, we're good." Lewis stood up and walked

confidently across the room. He was still well-dressed, flashy, and moved with a grace that wasn't usually associated with a drug house. He headed to the table on the opposite side of the room, where he picked up a joint and took one long, deep puff.

Miles waved to the two heavies, and they exited the room slowly, keeping their eyes locked on Harvey.

This wasn't a friendly house.

The two younger men who were playing the computer basketball video game turned off the television and scampered out of the room. They knew their place, and it wasn't in the middle of a discussion between the two heavyweights of the East L.A. drug trade. With his head held high and his shoulders drawn back, Lewis strolled back across the room to sink into the armchair, his long legs crossing over each other. Miles sat near him in another armchair, gesturing for Harvey to take a seat on the couch.

The couch had seen more drugs than a police evidence department, and he wondered if he'd get high just from sitting on it. Carefully, he sat on the couch as the two powerful men stared at him intently.

They didn't trust him. Even though he was trying to help their friend, they didn't have confidence in him.

Miles opened, staring directly at Harvey. "What do you want?"

"I want Carlos to get off these drug charges."

"It's all a setup," Miles added quickly. "All of it. Carlos hasn't touched drugs for years. He even tells us to get out of the game. Doesn't he, Juan?" Lewis didn't respond. "I know it wasn't him. It couldn't have been. He's a good man."

"If he has been out of the game, why are they after

PETER O'MAHONEY

him?" Harvey directed the question at Miles.

"You know why," Lewis snapped.

"You're due to appear tomorrow for the prosecution, right?" Harvey calmly asked an agitated Lewis.

"I'll be there in court. I don't have a choice. They said they would lock me up if I'm not in court tomorrow. So, yeah, I'll be there, but I won't like it."

"Once the prosecution has finished questioning you, I'll be asked if I wish to cross-examine you. This will be my opportunity to ask some questions that may help establish that Carlos is innocent. After we met last time, I sent you a list of questions. You never responded with your answers."

"I know the questions." Lewis uncrossed his legs, leaning forward on his knees. "And I know what I'm going to say. I don't need your help."

"Tell me what you want from me." Miles leaned forward as well. "Why are you here?"

The tension in the room was palpable.

Harvey took a moment to respond, looking at Lewis and then back to Miles.

He had planned to question Miles alone, but with Lewis present, he couldn't ask the questions he wanted.

He had to change his plan.

And he had to change it quickly.

"I was hoping that Lewis would be here. Not you, Roberto."

Miles' eyebrows rose to ask a question, looking across at Lewis.

"How did you know I was here?" Lewis grilled him.

"I'm a lawyer. I investigate. That's what I do.

144

That's what I do really well. And that's why I'm here."

"Are you saying that you were following me?" As a man who had lived his life as a criminal, Lewis never trusted a tail.

The last time he'd had a tail, the person went missing for five years. And the police only found his bones because developers began building on the site of an old empty car yard. 'Mauled to death by dogs,' the Los Angeles Coroner reported.

They weren't wrong.

"I wasn't following you, Lewis. I only assumed that you would be here."

Lewis didn't believe him.

His cold stare was only matched by Harvey's unflinching focus. To break a sweat here, to show one hint of nerves, would be suicide in this house.

He would go missing as well, and this time, Lewis would make sure that nobody would ever find the body.

"For Carlos' sake, I need to go over the questions that I sent you so there are no surprises in the courtroom. This is for your cousin's freedom. This isn't about you, and this isn't about me. This is about Carlos. This is about your family."

Lewis maintained the stare, waiting for a moment of unease from the attorney.

When it didn't come, he exhaled slowly, leaning back in his chair, and he looked across at Miles. Miles offered a small nod.

"Ask your questions." It was not a request; it was a demand.

"The prosecution is going to ask very direct questions about your relationship with Carlos and whether you have anything to do with supplying drugs. They're not going to sugarcoat any of the questions, so I need you to appear calm and honest in the face of their accusations."

"Of course."

Thinking on his feet was a skill that Harvey had always possessed. He had to. His choice of words had saved his life many times over.

"These questions will act as a warning shot for them. They're warning you that they're onto you and your operations. They want you to know that they're looking at your drug dealings, and they're not far away from catching you. They'll use this opportunity to pressure you on the stand to try and get you to slip up. Don't be surprised if they ask you very straightforward questions, one after the other. They're trying to catch you in a lie."

Lewis laughed. "They're a very long way from catching me. I know what questions they're going to ask, and my answers are already prepared. I'm ready for what they'll throw at me tomorrow. I have a lot of very powerful friends, and they'll always make sure that I'm one step ahead of the law."

The statement caught Harvey off guard. He was too confident. Too poised.

Something wasn't right.

"And if these powerful friends don't help you out?"

"Then they'll find out just how nasty I can be." Lewis gritted his teeth. "It's like I told my friend Carlos that morning when I was meeting with him in his apartment—if he just does what I ask, then nothing bad will come of it."

"Tell me why you needed Carlos to be an alibi before the raid had even happened?"

"I'm not telling you anything about that."

Lewis glanced at Miles, and Miles dropped his head.

"You just said that you were in the apartment that morning telling Carlos that you two were together all day, but that was before the raid. Either you knew about the raid, or you needed an alibi for something else. If you weren't at the diner meeting with Carlos, where were you?"

Lewis stared at Harvey intently. "I was taking care of business."

"Such as?"

"Does it matter?"

"It may be tomorrow when you're on the stand in court under oath."

"I don't care about being under oath. I'll be on that stand, and I'll say whatever I want."

"I hope you stick to the same story. If your story changes at any point during the testimony, the prosecution will destroy you. If they even get a hint that something is wrong or misplaced, then they'll attack you. If you give them the chance, then it'll be very dangerous for you and Carlos in the courtroom. I'll give you one word of advice for free, Lewis— make sure your house is clean tomorrow because if you slip up in the slightest, they'll raid it. If you give them the slightest opportunity, they'll exploit it. They want you behind bars."

Miles squinted as he stared at Harvey. "I hope you aren't thinking of doing anything stupid."

"I'm not a stupid man. My life has been spent dealing with criminals. I know what you can do."

A heavy silence drifted over the room.

"I have a lot of friends. A lot of powerful friends.

They wouldn't like it if anything happened to me. They wouldn't like it if I ended up behind bars." Lewis leaned forward again.

The pressure was building.

And Harvey didn't want to be there when it detonated.

Miles leaned his body slightly forward as well, defending his friend. "I think you're about to find out how friendly we can be."

It was time to leave.

Cautiously, Harvey stood and slowly walked to the exit. No sudden movements, but no hesitation.

"Tomorrow is going to be an interesting day, gentlemen. Be prepared."

CHAPTER 21

The walk from Harvey's car to the bar was a short one.

And that was just the way Harvey liked it.

He felt the strong need for a glass of whiskey after his chat with Lewis and Miles. Despite his flair, Lewis had an air of psychotic danger surrounding him. He had reportedly ordered the hit on as many as twenty people around his neighborhood, and he didn't regret it for one moment. He was as ruthless as he was stylish.

That made Harvey uneasy.

The more a criminal evaded the police, the more invincible they became.

The more crimes they committed and didn't get charged for, the closer they came to losing control.

Harvey was afraid that Lewis had already walked to the edge and lost restraint. The power had gone to Lewis' head, and he felt invincible. He felt he could get away with anything. He might be the king in his world, but he was stepping into a different territory. He held no power in court, and if he wasn't careful, the prosecution was going to tear him apart.

One wrong word from Lewis could destroy any chance Harvey had of getting Carlos off the charges.

Despite his past, Carlos López was a good man.

Harvey knew that. He wanted to help him. He wanted Carlos back on the street so he could help drug addicts recover.

The chill of the cool night air hit Harvey as he stepped out of the car.

After he stepped onto the sidewalk, he tossed a couple of dollars into the hat of a homeless man sitting nearby because he always felt that if things fell apart, that could easily be him. A few dollars didn't mean much to Harvey, but it meant the world to the homeless man.

When you live life so close to the edge, you have to be prepared to fall over it.

Harvey turned up his collar to the cold and damp and moved to lock his car door.

The moment he turned, he felt a large hand rest on his shoulder. Instinctively, he swung around.

He only had time to see a fist come towards his face.

The fist connected heavily with Harvey's cheekbone, throwing him back against his car.

His arms flew out sideways, trying to keep him upright, but he quickly landed on his behind, dazed by the surprise impact.

That wasn't a lucky punch.

This person knew exactly what they were doing.

As Harvey's head lifted off the pavement, two men grabbed him under his arms and dragged his body into the closest alley.

The fog cleared.

The adrenalin kicked in.

Harvey attempted to spring to his feet.

He wrestled free with his strength.

But there was another punch.

His world was dark.

Another fist connected with the back of his head. He didn't see that one.

Another fist.

He sprawled onto the pavement.

A boot.

The force connected with his ribs, and he curled up in pain. When another boot came towards him, his arm instinctively grabbed it.

Gripping the ankle tightly, he threw the man to the ground and leaped to his feet at the same time.

Having spent most of his childhood at a boxing gym, he knew how to throw a decent punch. When the second thug got close to him, he swung, and he swung hard.

They say in boxing that if you hit a man clean on the chin, he won't feel it until tomorrow.

As Harvey's heavy fist connected with the jaw of one of the thugs, he felt the satisfaction of it breaking under his force.

But that satisfaction didn't last long.

Another fist hit him in the ribs.

And another fist hit him in the back of the head.

Two more quick jabs into his body, and Harvey had landed heavily on the pavement.

A quick succession of boots.

He didn't stand a chance.

He tried to catch a glimpse of the attackers, but he was blinded by the barrage.

The taste of blood began to fill his mouth.

His vision began to blur.

Another hit.

Another one.

His head was spinning.

His arms flailed in a feeble attempt at defense. A heavy kick to his ribs robbed his lungs of any existing breath.

His resistance didn't last long.

Boot after boot landed on his body.

His efforts turned to protecting himself.

When his resistance had finished, the boots stopped flying.

Instinctively, Harvey grasped his wallet and held it against his chest.

"Don't go digging into the wrong business," the voice snarled at him, inches from his ear. "You'll find that people don't like you sniffing around in the wrong places. We'll be back if you don't stop digging."

Of course.

These men didn't want his wallet.

CHAPTER 22

The quiet darkness of the parking lot caused Kate Spencer to shudder.

She didn't trust the night. She never had.

When she was a small six-year-old girl, she'd watched as her mother and father were mugged and beaten under the darkness of a still night. She'd been overcome with fear as her father tried to fight back, struggling desperately to protect his family, but there were too many of them. She'd watched in terror as her father was kicked on the ground over and over again.

After months in the hospital, he was able to walk again, but his gait was never the same.

Nor was his personality.

Tonight, Kate could feel those same chills in the air. The small hairs on her arms stood on end.

She could sense the danger.

She knew it was there.

Despite her boss' desperate plea for her not to work late, she'd ignored his request. She loved her work—wanting to complete it before she went home to her empty house. Her son was with his deadbeat father for the next two days, and she couldn't bear the thought of sitting home alone.

Empty nesters claim they're the only ones who

know the grief of losing their children to adulthood, but for divorcees, that pain was just as real. Their family, their hopes and dreams, the people they had invested so much in, were suddenly gone, spending time somewhere else, laughing, crying, and growing.

It had taken Kate a long time to deal with that pain.

Every time her eight-year-old son left to go to her deadbeat ex-husband's apartment, she cried a pool of tears. Her son was growing up without her. Without her love. He was experiencing a life that she had no part in.

She didn't miss her ex-husband for one minute, not for one second, but she missed her son every waking minute that he wasn't with her. There was an emptiness in her heart, an ache that she couldn't cure. Over time, she had learned to ignore that pain, distracting herself with work.

Despite the years that had passed since her divorce, going home to an empty house still filled the single mother with dread.

Now, she regretted the decision to work late. She should have listened to her boss.

The nerves were already pumping through her veins; she could feel her own heartbeat against the walls of her chest. She could see every movement in her peripheral vision, seeing even the slightest break in the shadows.

Gripping her purse tightly in one hand, her keys in the other, she stepped towards her car, parked on the other side of the lot, a mere fifty yards away.

Her knuckles turned white with the force of her grip.

She stepped into the dark.

There was movement in the shadows.

She knew it.

She could see it.

But now, the distance between her car and the office door was the same. Twenty-five yards each way.

Each door was locked.

Neither would be easy access.

She was stuck. Vulnerable. Helpless. In a panic, she began to run towards her car. Heart pounding. Muscles clenched. Vision focused on her destination.

But then…

She was hit from behind. She fell to the asphalt. Clutching her purse, she turned to see her attacker.

The shadow was wearing a balaclava. Their face was completely covered.

And then…

A fist hit her in the face. And then another. Right above the eye.

She loosened her grip on the bag. They could take it. It was not worth her life. But they didn't touch her bag.

They didn't want it.

"Take it," Kate pleaded. "Take it."

They ignored her pleas.

And then…

Another fist.

Kate began sobbing, her tears mixed with blood, and the attacker stopped.

They raised their fist, but this time, the hooded person turned and walked away.

They didn't take her bag.

That wasn't their target.

CHAPTER 23

"Bill?" There was a desperate plea in Kate's voice.

"Kate. Kate! What's wrong?"

"Someone… someone… attacked me."

"What? Who? Are you ok? Are you hurt?"

"I'm… ok."

"Where are you?"

"I'm in the car, outside the police station on sixth. I don't want to get out of my car, Bill. How do I know it's safe out there? I don't trust the night." Her tears started flowing again.

After her attacker left her bloodied on the pavement, Kate had focused on getting into her car, locking the doors, starting the engine, and racing to the nearest police station. It was only once she'd arrived that she let her guard down. It was only once she felt safe that she let the tears come.

"Kate, wait there. Keep the doors locked and the engine running. I'll be there in ten minutes. Don't get out of the car."

With a swollen face and still spitting blood, Harvey frantically raced to the station.

When he arrived, he saw her car, engine running, lights on, exhaust fumes slowly escaping into the chill of the night air.

Carefully, he approached her driver's side window.

She was gripping the steering wheel tightly, staring straight ahead.

Seeing dried blood on her face sent anger pulsing through his body.

He had let her down. He should have protected her, but he'd let her down.

Gently, he tapped on the driver's side window.

Kate turned her head, taking a few seconds to process who was standing by her car. When she finally realized it was Harvey, she leaped out, embracing him in a tight hug.

He held her tight. He let her safety be threatened. He couldn't forgive himself for that.

"Are you sure you're ok? Should we get you to the hospital?"

"I'm not hurt." She wiped the wetness from her eyes, sniffing back more tears.

"What happened?"

"In the parking lot, after work, someone jumped me between the office and the car."

"At our office?" Another wave of guilt washed over Harvey. That was his office. The place he should be able to ensure was safe. "What were you doing there so late?"

"I was looking for the delivery date of the new armchair like you asked. I got it, Bill. The armchair was delivered the morning Judge Hardgrave was shot."

He'd put the woman he cared for in danger. "That doesn't matter now. What matters is that you're ok. What matters is that you're fine."

"They didn't want my purse, Bill. I told them to take it, but they didn't want it. Why didn't they take my purse?"

Anger continued to consume Harvey's thoughts.

This wasn't a random attack. This wasn't a coincidence.

This was a targeted assault.

For both him and Kate.

"Did you get a look at them?"

"No, not really. It all happened so fast, and they were wearing a balaclava. They didn't want to be seen."

"Anything? Did you see anything about them? Anything at all."

"The only thing I saw was that one of them was wearing a blue and green love heart necklace. It was tight around their neck, but the shine of the love heart caught my eye. That's all I saw."

Harvey hugged Kate tightly again.

He had seen the necklace before.

He knew who it belonged to.

As they hugged, they melted into each other, and Harvey started to feel it.

He didn't want to, but he could feel the emotion building inside him.

His father had been the same. He hadn't wanted emotions in his life. He'd only wanted to do his job, provide for his family, and watch football on Sunday with a beer in his hand. He didn't want to be drawn into the weakness of emotions. He didn't want to be suckered into feeling something.

That was the only way Harvey had learned to deal with emotions. It was all he'd known as he grew up. His only male role model had avoided showing his feelings at all costs.

"Caring for something will make you weak, boy," his father had told him over and over. When Harvey was only six years old, he still hugged his pink teddy bear every night. He loved that teddy bear, a present from his late grandmother. His father had torn it away from him on the night of his sixth birthday and told him that it was time to grow up. The thing he'd loved the most was torn away by the person he respected the most.

A brick wall had been built around Harvey's heart ever since.

For him, caring was a flaw.

But now, as he gripped this woman tight, he couldn't resist it. That brick wall couldn't hold back the flood of emotion any longer.

He should have protected Kate.

He should have been there for her.

And it hurt him more than anything that he'd put her in danger.

"What happened to you?" Kate asked as she looked up at Harvey's face.

"I just walked into the wrong area at the wrong time," he lied. "Come on, Kate. Let's get to the station and make a report."

She rested against his chest as they walked to the station doors, but Harvey's thoughts were elsewhere.

He was thinking about the owner of that necklace.

CHAPTER 24

"What happened to you?" Detective Matthew Pitt opened his front door and looked at his old friend in surprise.

Bill Harvey was standing on the doorstep, dried blood on his lip, a cut above his swollen eye. He was holding his side tightly with his left hand and leaning on his other side. His broken ribs hurt, but there was nothing that the hospital could do about that.

And he didn't have time to waste.

"I just had a quiet chat with the wrong people." Harvey's response was firm.

"Come in." Pitt opened the door.

Harvey limped in, short of breath.

"Bev, get the first aid kit," Pitt called out to his wife.

Pitt's wife rushed down the stairs of their house with the first aid kit in hand. "Oh, Bill," she sighed. "You just can't stay out of trouble, can you?"

"It finds me, Bev." Harvey smiled with a split front lip. "I don't go looking for it; it just comes and tracks me down."

She smiled, took Harvey into the kitchen, and spent the next ten minutes cleaning up his cuts, making small talk along the way.

"But clearly." She sighed as she finished cleaning

his cuts. "You didn't come here for my nursing skills. I know that I have a delicate touch, but a handsome man like you can get that anywhere. I'll let you two boys chat. But Bill, promise me one thing?"

"What's that, Bev?"

"Stay out of trouble, or next time, it'll be me giving you a cut lip." She gently placed her hand on his face before leaving the room.

"I'd listen to her," Pitt joked. "I tell you, if I make that woman angry, there are some nights I sleep with one eye open."

"I heard that," Bev called out from down the hall.

Once Bev was out of earshot, Harvey stared at Pitt, who was resting against the kitchen counter.

"I wasn't the only one targeted."

"Who else?"

"Kate."

"No." Pitt's shock was real. "Is she hurt?"

"She's a little shaken up, but she's going to be ok. She's at my place now." After the evening that Harvey had endured, he was in no mood for further small talk. "You need to tell me the truth, and you need to tell it to me now."

"About what?" Pitt squinted his eyes.

"About you and Miles."

Pitt opened his mouth in surprise. He shouldn't be shocked. The lawyer standing in front of him was known for his investigative skills just as much as he was known for tearing a person apart on the stand.

Harvey held Pitt's stare, and Pitt acknowledged it with a few small nods. Slowly, he turned to the kitchen door and closed it gently. Walking back to the counter, he sat down on the stool opposite his friend.

"Start talking."

"Roberto Miles…" Pitt sighed. "He's a big player in the drug scene in East L.A.—Juan Lewis' partner in the scene. We've been after him for years, trying to land something big on him. But all we ever get is something small, a charge that's just big enough to keep him off the streets for a little while. After he does time in prison, he's straight back out on the streets, helping Lewis in the drug import trade. But then, he ran into big trouble with the law and with me."

"And?"

"And he struck a deal with us. He was going to give us Lewis, and we would ignore the charges. Lewis is the main player out there. He's the brains behind the operations, and without him, the whole thing would fall apart. So, although we could get Miles, it wouldn't have stopped the drug operations. We wanted to get Lewis."

"Miles will just step into the position once Lewis is gone."

Pitt nodded. "We thought about that. That's why we have an old case that we can convict Miles on as well. He doesn't know that. Nobody does. We're going to nail Lewis, and then we're going to nail Miles. Roberto Miles isn't the smartest guy going around. You could tell him that the sun is computer-programmed by Bill Gates, and he would believe you. The plan is that he'll give us Lewis, and then we will nail him a week later on the old charge."

"Except you haven't nailed Lewis with anything. He's as free as a bird."

"You're right. We haven't got anything yet. Miles is wired a lot of the time, but we haven't got anything. Nothing."

"He's playing you. I have word that a large run of drugs is coming in soon."

"Possibly."

"What's the old case you have with Miles?"

"I can't say, Harvey. I can't let you know that. Just know that it's big."

Harvey nodded slowly, processing the information. "Matthew, I need a favor."

"Of course. I thought that was the reason you might be here. But as much as you're a friend, it depends on what the favor is. These are treacherous times."

"I need you in court tomorrow."

"What for?"

"I have a hunch, and I'm going to make a play."

Pitt laughed. "Your hunches have gotten me into trouble before, Bill. A lot of trouble. I'm not sure what to make of that request."

"They may have gotten you into trouble, but we've always gotten the criminal. Don't tell me that you've changed your story, and now you don't want the criminal? I thought all the police wanted was for the guilty to pay—you worry about the details later."

"Very true." Pitt sighed and pulled out a cold beer from the fridge to pass to Harvey. "This should help your lip."

"I need someone in court that I can trust. I've got a big-time drug dealer coming to the stand, and under cross-examination, I plan to get him to admit he committed a crime. I need someone in the courtroom who isn't connected to his syndicate of high-powered contacts."

"Juan Lewis is on the stand tomorrow?"

Harvey nodded slowly.

"Be careful… although I can imagine that's probably why you have a cut lip right now, so you don't need me to tell you how dangerous he can be." Pitt took a long drink of his beer. "He's got friends in high places. Very high places. He can get away with a lot of stuff. If you're going to take him down, you have to take him down hard. Don't do this for a little play. Even if you pin that $50,000 worth of heroin on him, it won't keep him off the streets for long. If he walks away, he can have you hit the second you walk out on the street, and they can brush it under the carpet. With the level of protection that he has, you have to be very, very sure of what you're doing. It has to be a play that's going to take him off the streets forever."

"It appears that he's quite a dangerous person." Harvey gestured to his cuts and bruises. "But that shouldn't stop men like you and me. We have to be better than that, Pitt. We have to be above the fear that they want to instill in us. This is when courage counts."

"That's a lovely speech," Pitt replied. "But I'm not some officer fresh off the street. I know what pain is. And so do you. You've seen it before. You've seen the worst of it. We have people to protect now. I can't risk my family for this—because that's what will happen. They'll come after my family."

"Don't get scared on me now."

"Even what you and I have seen in the past isn't going to compare to what Lewis can do. His connection to Judge Hardgrave opened a lot of doors, and when a man like Lewis sees an open door, he jumps right through it. We know that he has anger issues—he'll snap if you push him."

"That's why I need you."

"Bill, because you're my friend, I'll be there. But we have to be clear with each other. This needs to be a really big play to take down Lewis. Really big. If you're going to take him down, make it count."

"I'm going to make a play so big that no one is going to want to go near him. Everyone will disown him. The people who protect him won't want to be associated with him anymore. They'll distance themselves from him very, very quickly."

"If you don't get this right, he'll come down on you even heavier than last time. On both you and Kate. You're risking your lives here."

"I know what's at risk." He looked Pitt up and down, judging his old clothes. "And wear a nice suit. You might be on television tomorrow."

"Is this play foolproof?"

"No. It's risky. Very risky."

"That's what I was afraid of."

CHAPTER 25

The second morning of the trial hummed along smoothly. Chettle did her best to present the circumstantial evidence, and Harvey did his best to dispute it. Like an unhappily married couple, they went back and forth for hours, arguing at any chance they got.

Standard procedure for a morning in court. Nothing special.

But all that was about to change as Chettle called Juan Lewis to the stand. She even shuddered when she called his name. She knew how important this testimony would be.

For the prosecution, it was about applying pressure. They needed to increase the pressure on the major drug supplier. They needed him to know that they were coming after him. He was their target.

As he walked with confidence through the courtroom, the case was balanced slightly in the prosecution's favor.

Lewis presented himself well—his suit was bright enough to force people to look twice, his hair slicked to the back and left, and his accessories were glittering under the lights. It almost seemed appropriate for Lewis to moonwalk to the witness stand.

As he walked past the defense table, one accessory

caught Bill Harvey's eye—a blue and green love heart necklace hanging around his neck, resting between the open collar of his shirt.

Harvey's leg twitched nervously under the defense table. He knew it was time. Time to make a play to win this case, but more importantly it was time to ensure Kate was kept safe.

He couldn't risk her life again.

His heart wouldn't take it.

Lewis was sworn in, and Chettle opened with her questions. "Mr. Juan Lewis, how long have you known Mr. Carlos López?"

"Many, many years." He winked at the prosecutor. "And may I just say that you look mighty fine today, lady."

"Mr. Lewis," Judge Windsor's voice echoed around the courtroom. "I will remind you that this is a courtroom, not a bar where you pick up women. Please save your sleazy comments for another place and respectfully answer the question that has been asked of you."

Lewis grinned, full of self-assurance. "Certainly, judge."

"Are you related to Mr. López?"

"I am. He's my cousin."

"Would you say that you and Mr. López are close?"

"Yes, we are. We have lunch or coffee every week."

"Every week?" Chettle questioned from behind her desk, reading from the notes in front of her. "How long have you been doing that?"

"Most of our adult lives, on and off."

"So you know a lot about Mr. López's life?"

"I do."

The answers were coming too quickly.

Gripping his pen tightly, Harvey prepared for a new turn in the case.

"On the day of September 12, the day of the raid on his apartment, where were you?"

"I was with Carlos López all day."

"Can you please explain to the court what happened on the day that the raid occurred at Mr. López's apartment?"

"I met with Carlos at his apartment in the morning, and we went to have lunch at one of our favorite diners, El Mejor. We stayed there for many hours, as we often do, and talked about life, love, and the future. After lunch, we stopped at a shop, and then we left to return to his apartment. When we returned to his car, he parked in the lot next door to his apartment building. I said goodbye to him, and he entered the apartment building alone. He later informed me that it was then that he was arrested."

Harvey felt the tension rise in the room.

"At any point during that day, did you see Carlos with this briefcase?" Chettle pointed to the case on the evidence table.

No…

Suddenly, it all fell into place for Harvey.

They'd been played—by Lewis and by the prosecution.

Lewis looked at the defense table and drew a deep breath.

"I did."

Carlos' mouth dropped open.

This wasn't part of their plan.

This wasn't part of their game.

Carlos clearly didn't expect his cousin to set him up.

Despite the suddenness of the accusation, Chettle didn't look the least bit surprised. She'd known this was coming.

She'd organized this.

"And please explain to the court when you saw Carlos with the briefcase?" she continued.

"When I met Carlos at his apartment that morning, he had the briefcase in his hand. He seemed nervous about it, almost like he didn't want me to know about it. When I suggested that we go out for lunch, he made sure he put the briefcase in a secure place in his bedroom. I wanted to ask him what was in the briefcase because he seemed so nervous about it, but I figured it was actually none of my business. He left it in his bedroom while we went out for lunch."

Lewis was living up to his promise about only saying the things in his best interest.

"Have you ever seen Carlos López take drugs?"

"In the past, yes."

"And does that bother you? Does it bother you that he has taken drugs before?"

"He made mistakes in his past, and that's fine with me. His crimes didn't affect me directly because I don't like drugs." He tried hard to hide his devilish grin, but he couldn't, no matter how much he wanted to. "However, I'm a forgiving man. I have looked past those dealings because my cousin Carlos has a good heart. He has a strong heart. And I honestly thought that he was done with the game. I thought that he was through with it. But we all know that dealing large quantities of drugs like that is a way to make a lot of money fast. I guess he needed the money and saw this as the quickest way to get it."

"It doesn't bother you that you spend a lot of time with a drug user?"

"Like I said, I have forgiven him for his sins. I wouldn't have any friends left if I didn't forgive people. We all make mistakes, lady."

Harvey could see the prosecution's play clearly.

They had struck a deal with Lewis.

When Carlos didn't roll over on his friend, Lewis became their main focus. They had tailed him, harassed him, and questioned him. Lewis must have given them something good to strike this deal.

The problem with making a deal with a man like Juan Lewis was that he would never pull back from the drug trade. This deal would only fuel his ego.

He would go bigger.

Faster.

Walking away from this courtroom would only increase his confidence.

"And have you ever been involved in the drug trade?"

"No."

"Mr. Lewis, can you please advise the court whether you ever saw Mr. López dealing drugs?"

"No, I didn't. I never saw Carlos deal or sell drugs, but I'm very well aware that he spent time in prison for drug crimes."

"Objection," Harvey called out. "Past convictions—"

"Withdrawn," Chettle responded quickly, but the damage was already done. "Thank you, Mr. Lewis. No further questions."

As he stared at the paper in front of him, the sweat

collected on Harvey's brow.

Not only was he fighting for the safety of Kate Spencer and fighting a now almost impossible case, but he was also fighting a lying drug dealer.

He thought about this morning when he saw Kate at the office, a bandage on her chin, black eye still visible. His eyes then turned to Carlos, a man with a troubled past but who was clearly innocent of the charges.

Justice or safety?

Should he go after Lewis and risk Kate? Or should he let Carlos go to prison and keep Kate safe?

Justice or safety?

A question he could not answer.

CHAPTER 26

After the shock of Juan Lewis' accusation, Judge Windsor called for a short recess, a chance for the defense to think about how they could possibly put their case back together.

As soon as Harvey stepped out of the courtroom, Carlos grabbed his arm firmly.

They stood in the hallway of the courthouse, each of them confused about what had just happened. They didn't see it coming. The hallway was empty, except for the people racing through to another case, and they felt a moment of relief from the intensity of the courtroom.

"What just happened?" Carlos asked, shaking his head.

"It appears that your cousin, Juan Lewis, has just pinned the case on you. He didn't want to go down for the crime, so he's heaping all the blame on you. I didn't expect that. I didn't expect that he would do that. He must have struck a good deal with the prosecution."

"Why would he have struck a deal with the prosecution? Why would they have let him do that?"

"He must be going to sell someone out…" Harvey reasoned as he talked the situation through. "It must be Miles. That's the only thing he could offer them.

He'll get immunity from the charges. But Pitt has already struck a deal with Roberto Miles."

"And the prosecution has struck a deal with Lewis?"

"Lewis and Miles are double-crossing each other." Harvey ran his hand through his hair. "They're both trying to sell each other out to take over the business. They've both turned on each other."

"That's trouble, Bill. Lewis is bad, but Miles would beat up his own mother if it got him another cookie. He's relentlessly violent. When he finds out that Lewis has turned on him for a deal, he'll be unstoppable."

"Your trouble right now is that your cousin, someone you thought you could trust, has just sold you out. That must have been part of the deal as well."

"But why would he do that? We're like brothers, and he knows the briefcase wasn't mine. He lied in there."

The pain in his eyes was clear. Nothing was more important to him than family, and he had never thought his own family could do that to him.

"The prosecution must have found something on Lewis. They must have got him into a room and squeezed him tight. He must have felt the pressure. That's what they wanted to happen. They wanted to break him. He must have struck a deal to turn over on Miles, and they want you to go down for this crime. Your relationship means very little to him right now. His freedom means so much more."

"That wasn't my briefcase. He knows that. He's lying about that briefcase."

"I'm sure it wasn't yours. I believe you, Carlos.

One hundred percent. But it's not up to me; it's up to the jury to make that decision. And right now, they're all thinking that you owned the briefcase. Even the jurors who were sitting on the fence before now look convinced after that little play from Lewis. A witness has stated that they saw you with the briefcase. That's the hook, line, and sinker for these jurors."

Tears welled up in Carlos' eyes as he huffed out all the pain and leaned against the hallway wall. He loosened his tie, and the back of his head tapped against the wall as he tried to understand what had just happened.

His cousin had sold him out. He was about to go back to prison.

With a hefty sigh, his head dropped towards the floor. "If I leave now, I can make a run for the border."

"It's not over yet, Carlos."

"What are you talking about?" Carlos' eyes squinted together. "It's over. Didn't you hear what he said in there?"

"I have one play left."

"What do you mean?"

"I need to get under his skin. I need to make Lewis angry. He has an anger management problem, and I need to exploit that." Harvey leaned close to Carlos. "Lewis is about to send you to prison, so I need you to tell me something that'll get under his skin. Is there anything that will make Lewis furious? Anything that can get under his skin?"

"Maybe."

"Come on, Carlos. Tell me."

"Michelle Hardgrave."

"What about Michelle?"

"This last year, they have had a very on-again, off-again relationship. They're together at the moment. They hate each other, and then five minutes later, they love each other. It's been a volatile year for them. If you mention her, bring her into this; it might make Lewis angry."

"How long have they been back together?"

"Probably a week before my arrest." Carlos rubbed his brow. "He would do anything for her. Anything. He doesn't want to lose Michelle. If you threaten her, then it'll push his buttons. If you make a threat against her, he'll get really angry. He won't be able to hold himself back."

"That may be enough to get under his skin," Harvey responded, thinking about his next step.

"I'm done, aren't I? There's no coming back from here, is there? Lewis has made sure that I'm going down for this crime. I can tell." Carlos' eyes showed a lot of pain. "I can't go back to prison, Bill. You can't let that happen to me. I'm innocent. I can't go to prison because I'm innocent. That's the way this system is supposed to work."

"I wouldn't give up just yet."

"There's nothing left, Bill. Nothing. There is nothing more that we can do. I should go now. Tonight. Make a run for the border. I could cross without anyone knowing. Run the tunnels. On the other side, I have family. They are a real family, not like Lewis. They'll look after me. Help me set up my life down there. It wouldn't be much, but it would be better than prison. I can't do that again."

Harvey placed a consoling hand on Carlos' shoulder. "Carlos, I have one play left. I'm going to question Lewis next, and it's going to get hot in there."

"What if it doesn't work?"

"Then nowhere is going to be safe for either of us."

CHAPTER 27

After the jurors were ushered back into the courtroom, Harvey had his chance to question drug baron Juan Lewis.

Lewis rested on the witness stand, waiting for the questions, looking supremely poised.

When prosecutor Shannon Chettle had called him and offered him a deal five days ago, he'd jumped at the chance. She had evidence that connected him to a smaller drug deal, but if he sold out his partner, Roberto Miles, and his cousin, Carlos López, she would be willing to discuss a deal.

She'd given him immunity from the new charges in exchange for evidence against Miles and testimony against López. For Chettle, it wasn't personal. She didn't care who went to prison; she just wanted the drugs off the streets. She saw the impending arrest of Miles and the charge against López as victories.

She knew about Detective Pitt's offer to Miles to set up Lewis, but that had been two months in the making. Here, she had two wins in quick succession. Big wins. Wins big enough to put her name in the paper.

What she didn't know was that Lewis was the worst of the lot.

And she had only fueled his ego.

After he was called to begin his questioning, Bill Harvey contemplated the case at the desk, thinking over the last chance that lay before him.

"Mr. Lewis," he began. "Can you please confirm where you were on September 12?"

Lewis stared at Harvey with a flashy smile. "As I have stated previously, I was with Carlos López all day."

"But you weren't at the El Mejor diner with Carlos López that day, were you?"

"Yes, I was."

"Really? I have evidence to prove that you weren't there. So, I'll ask you again, where were you?"

Lewis didn't answer; instead, his eyes stared straight at Harvey.

"Mr. Lewis, please answer the question," Judge Windsor prompted Lewis to answer.

"There is no evidence of that because it's not true. It can't be true because we were together all day. All day. Isn't that right, Carlos?" Lewis stared at his cousin.

"The defense would like to introduce new evidence to the court—the security footage of the El Mejor diner for September 12."

The body language of Lewis changed. He leaned forward, crossing his arms, subconsciously protecting himself from the attack.

"Look," Lewis argued before the footage was presented. "Maybe we got the diner wrong. Carlos and I frequent a lot of diners around town, and maybe we got our diners mixed up. Maybe we weren't at the El Mejor diner that day. Maybe we made a mistake about which diner we were at on that day."

"So, despite your sworn testimony that you were at

the El Mejor diner, are you now changing that? Which diner were you at that day, Mr. Lewis?" Harvey asked, staring straight at Lewis.

"Maybe we were there. Maybe we weren't. I'm not sure. I don't keep a diary of every daily event, so I have nothing to check. All I know is that we were at a diner that day. Sometimes, people can get confused."

"Or maybe you're lying?"

"No." Lewis was starting to become agitated with Harvey's line of questioning. "I know for sure that we were together. That's the truth."

"Were you with your girlfriend that day, Mr. Lewis?" Harvey enquired loudly.

"On that day, I didn't have a girlfriend," Lewis stated as his jaw clenched.

"Really?" Harvey faked his surprise. "I thought you were dating Michelle Hardgrave? Daughter of Judge Andrew Hardgrave?"

Lewis' nostrils flared. "I am."

"But not on that day?"

"No."

"Objection," Chettle called out. "This information isn't relevant to the case."

"Your Honor," Harvey explained. "I'm merely trying to establish where this witness was during the day in question."

"Overruled," Judge Windsor stated. "Continue the questioning, but get to the point quickly, Mr. Harvey."

As Harvey reviewed his notes, Lewis gripped the arm of his chair tightly, breathing heavily through his nostrils. He had been warned by Chettle that the defense would try and make him angry, so he'd taken pre-emptive action—he quickly smoked two joints before he entered the courthouse.

But even that wasn't helping him right now.

Harvey had certainly pushed the right button.

Harvey paused for a few long moments, creating an uncomfortable silence, and then continued, "If you weren't with Michelle Hardgrave on that day, can you tell us the last time you saw her?"

"Objection," Chettle called out again. "I fail to see how this is relevant."

"Overruled. Get to the point, Mr. Harvey," Judge Windsor repeated.

"She dumped you, didn't she? Her father finally got her clean and off the drugs, and when she was clean, she dumped you. That must have hurt, Mr. Lewis."

"Objection. The defense—"

"Withdrawn," Harvey stated, standing up to begin pacing the floor of the courtroom. He could see the fire in Lewis' eyes.

Ready to snap.

Just where Harvey wanted him.

"Mr. Lewis, Carlos López didn't have the briefcase on that day, did he?"

"Yes, he did."

"But you never saw him with it, did you?"

"Yes, I did."

He closed the gap between Lewis and himself.

"Have you ever dealt drugs, Mr. Lewis?" Harvey caught a glimpse of a confused look on Chettle's face. She had no idea what he was playing at.

"No."

"Have you ever taken drugs?"

Lewis's voice rose as he became increasingly frustrated. "No."

"Have you ever been tempted to take drugs?"

"What is this?!" Lewis fired back.

Usually, Harvey would expect an objection to this line of questioning, but Chettle didn't look like she was going to object any time soon. She felt like the line of questioning was working in her favor.

Judge Windsor looked to the prosecution, almost pleading with her to object, but when she didn't, he stated, "Please answer the questions asked of you, Mr. Lewis."

"No," Lewis snapped. "I have never been tempted to take drugs!"

"Have you ever watched anyone take drugs?"

"What is this?" Lewis replied angrily.

"Please answer the questions," Judge Windsor stated again.

"No!"

"Did Michelle take drugs?"

"No!"

"Objection. Not relevant."

"Did you give her drugs, Lewis?!"

"No!"

"Your Honor. Objection!"

"You gave her drugs, didn't you?!"

"No!"

"Mr. Harvey!" Judge Windsor boomed.

"She only loved you for the drugs, Lewis!"

"Objection! Not relevant to this case! There is no established connection between Michelle Hardgrave and this case!"

"Sustained!"

"She didn't love you, Lewis! She loved the drugs!"

"The objection is sustained, Mr. Harvey! You will stop that line of questioning immediately!"

"Withdrawn, Your Honor."

"Stick to the current case, Mr. Harvey!" Judge Windsor's eyes narrowed as he stared at the defense attorney.

Harvey moved back to his table to review his notes. "That's a nice tie, Mr. Lewis."

"It is." He adjusted his tie in the middle of his shirt.

"You like your ties, don't you?"

"I do."

"You like to have a little bit of flair, a little bit of color, don't you?"

"It's my style. It makes me who I am. Just because I wear nice ties doesn't mean I'm a criminal." The tone of Lewis' voice was understandably frustrated.

"You were wearing that tie last time I saw you, and you mentioned that Judge Hardgrave also liked that tie."

"He loved it. He had an armchair that was exactly the same color. I sat in his orange armchair, and this tie blended right in."

"Blended into a purple armchair?"

"No, man. Orange."

"Orange?"

"That's what I said." The arrogance and anger flowed from his words. "Are you stupid?"

"Are you certain it was orange?"

"Yes." Lewis squinted his eyebrows in confusion.

"When was the last time you saw Judge Hardgrave?"

"Objection," Chettle called out. "Again, I fail to see how this is relevant to the case."

"Mr. Harvey?" Judge Windsor asked.

"I assure you, Your Honor, that this is very

relevant to the date of the alleged crime in the current case."

"Overruled, but you're at the limit. Don't push me, Mr. Harvey." Judge Windsor nodded, letting the questioning continue to satisfy his curiosity. "Please answer the question, Mr. Lewis."

"Three days before his death."

Harvey's voice rose. "And when was the last time you were in his living room?"

"The same time."

"Really?"

"Yes."

"In his living room?! He made that comment about liking your tie?" Harvey's hand slammed down on the defense table.

"Yes!"

"Because that bright orange armchair wasn't delivered until the day of his death, which also happens to be September 12 when you were not with my client in the El Mejor diner! So, I will ask you again." Harvey's voice boomed aggression. "Mr. Lewis, where were you on September 12?!"

"I said—"

"Mr. Lewis! I put it to you that you were not with my client on September 12, but you were with Judge Hardgrave at that time!"

"I—"

"Mr. Lewis! The only way you could have known the color of the armchair was orange, like your tie, were if you were there that day!"

"I—"

"Mr. Lewis! You're under oath!"

"I…" Lewis stammered.

"Mr. Lewis! You were with Judge Hardgrave! Not

Carlos!"

"No."

"Mr. Lewis! You are under oath!"

"So what?!"

"Mr. Lewis! You were with Judge Hardgrave that day!"

"Whatever! So what if I was with Hardgrave that day! That doesn't prove anything!"

"You shot him."

"No!"

"Mr. Lewis! You shot Judge Hardgrave and planned to use Carlos López as your alibi!"

"No!"

"Except your plan didn't include the fact that Carlos' apartment was being raided that morning for your drugs!"

"Not my drugs!" Lewis began to falter under the shock of the accusation.

"Mr. Lewis! You shot Judge Hardgrave because he wasn't going to give you any more money! He wanted nothing more to do with you!"

"I-"

"He hated you!" Harvey snarled. "And his daughter hated you! She dumped you! She hated you, Lewis!"

"No!"

"You shot her father in cold blood!"

"No!"

"You shot him!"

"So what?! I shot the prick!" Lewis finally snapped. Harvey had pushed the right buttons.

"Yeah, I shot him. I shot him up close. Real close. I saw the blood splatter everywhere. I hated that guy. He deserved it."

The courtroom erupted into a commotion.

The noise was overwhelming.

"Order! Order!"

When Lewis realized that his anger had gotten the better of him, he sunk back into the chair, his mouth wide open.

He couldn't control his anger.

And it had just cost him his freedom.

"You killed Judge Andrew Hardgrave on the same day that you claim to have seen my client with the briefcase."

"I…" Lewis held his words. "I didn't say that."

"You did. You just said it. You're on record saying that, Juan Lewis. This is a court of law, and every statement is recorded."

"Your Honor." Chettle was frantic. "The prosecution calls for an adjournment."

Judge Windsor looked to the detectives standing at the back of the room, ready to arrest Juan Lewis for the murder of Judge Andrew Hardgrave. "In light of this testimony, I think that's a very wise decision."

"Lewis, you killed my friend. You will go to prison for a very long time." Harvey snarled.

"Mr. Harvey," Judge Windsor boomed. "We're done with questioning now. In light of this new confession, the court has to recess."

"But I'm not done questioning yet." Harvey looked up to the Judge.

"For now, you are. The court is adjourned!"

Detective Matthew Pitt, dressed in his finest suit, walked from the back of the courtroom to the witness stand. He read Juan Lewis his Miranda rights for the murder of Judge Andrew Hardgrave.

"Do you have anything to say, Juan Lewis?" Pitt

placed handcuffs on the witness.

"I was alone," Juan Lewis called out loud enough for the entire courtroom to hear.

The random statement caught Harvey by surprise.

He stared at Lewis, but he avoided eye contact.

"I was alone," he repeated loudly.

Then, the reality hit Bill Harvey.

It hit him like a truck.

This wasn't over yet.

Juan Lewis didn't murder Judge Andrew Hardgrave.

And a dangerous killer was still free.

CHAPTER 28

With frantic energy, Bill Harvey raced from the courthouse. Aggressively, he pushed past the media throng that had assembled and jumped straight into the nearest cab.

Desperately, he called his office repeatedly.

"Pick up, Kate. Pick up."

She didn't.

When the cab arrived at his office door, Bill Harvey almost fell out of the cab, anxious to get to the office before anyone else.

"Kate!" he yelled, racing through the door. "Kate!"

As she sat at her desk, innocently about to grab a bite to eat, she looked at the desperate man in front of her.

"What is it, Bill? What's wrong?"

"It wasn't a man that hit you."

"What do you mean?"

"It was a woman."

"Who?"

Harvey pulled the phone out of his pocket. "The most dangerous person involved in this mess is still out there. She's free. This isn't over yet, Kate. I have to find your attacker before she does it again. As soon as she hears about Lewis going to prison, she'll want revenge. And she might be coming after you."

"Who? Who am I avoiding, Bill?" She was panicking. "I thought I was avoiding Lewis. What about the necklace? Didn't you say that the necklace belonged to Lewis?"

Harvey's eyes thinned with acknowledgment of the truth. "It's not Lewis."

"But the necklace?"

"That necklace is a lover's necklace. You take one half, and your lover takes the other."

"But Lewis would have—"

"Lewis isn't the murderer, either."

"Then who is?"

Harvey turned to the door and locked it.

"Michelle Hardgrave."

CHAPTER 29

"Jack," Harvey yelled into his phone. "I need to find Michelle Hardgrave. Now."

"Good luck with that one, buddy."

"Why?"

"She has no fixed address, and nobody is going to tell you where to find her. You'll have no luck locating her."

"You must know something. Anything."

"If I knew anything, Harvey, I would tell you, but I don't. Your best bet would be to look at one of Lewis' homes. Maybe she's there. What's the rush?"

Without answering the question, Harvey hung up the phone and turned to Kate. "I want you to go straight away and get Connor. Go to your mother's house. Don't stop for anything. Once you're at your mother's house, don't go out. Lock the doors and keep Connor inside. This woman is dangerous, Kate."

"But Bill—"

"No, Kate. This isn't the time to argue."

As he talked, the phone buzzed in his pocket.

An unknown number.

If this was a telemarketer, Harvey would tear them apart on the phone.

"Bill Harvey," he answered.

"Bill Harvey, this is Michelle Hardgrave."

"Michelle Hardgrave?" His eyes squinted as he looked at Kate. "How can I help you?"

"I have a job for you. I need you to sign a document. Meet me at the Vincent Thomas Bridge in thirty minutes. Bring a pen."

CHAPTER 30

The bridge was only twenty-five minutes away by cab, and Harvey wasted no time organizing a ride. This wasn't a job for a new Uber driver; this was the time for a lifelong cabbie who knew the L.A. streets like the back of his hand. He threw a fifty at the cabbie and told him to drive faster than he had ever driven before.

The back seat of the cab was dirty, smelly, and rotten, but that made no difference now. His only focus was his destination.

Gripping the door tightly, he stared out the window, trying to understand why Michelle Hardgrave would want to meet him at the Vincent Thomas Bridge.

It wasn't the place to assault someone. It wasn't the place to commit murder. If Michelle wanted to do that, she would have asked him to meet in a more secluded area, perhaps a warehouse. This was no quiet area.

But it also wasn't the place to conduct a public-style execution. Not enough people to witness the event. If she wanted that, she would have done it on the courthouse steps.

He felt safe but wary.

"Stop!" he yelled to the cabbie as they approached the bridge. He jumped out of the car, tossing a few more bills into the front seat.

Standing at the end of the bridge, looking towards the swollen river below, was the lone figure of Michelle Hardgrave.

Her hair blew gently in the breeze, and for the first time, Harvey saw the resemblance to her father. The same broad shoulders. The same lean legs.

Holding a piece of paper tightly, she stared out to the river. Cautiously, Harvey approached her.

"Michelle Hardgrave."

Slowly, she turned away from the river, looking at the man approaching. Her mini-skirt was old and dirty; her denim jacket was the same.

"He isn't a good man." There was a reflection in her voice, the voice of a woman well-educated but with the edge of someone who had lived their life on the streets.

"Your father did a lot of great things in this world, Michelle. He helped a lot of people."

She looked back to the river. Her hair was dry and brittle from dehydration, and her skin looked the same. Her body looked like the water had been slowly sucked from it. She was a beautiful girl once, a girl with the world at her feet. Now, she looked ten years older than she was, with some teeth missing and the whites of her eyes almost glowing yellow.

Only her blue and green love heart necklace appeared well looked after.

"I was talking about Juan."

"I can't speak for Juan Lewis. I don't know him."

"He's going to prison, isn't he?"

"For a very long time, Michelle."

Turning to face Harvey, she looked contemplative, pensive—the same look that her father often had.

"He was a very horrible man as well." Michelle scratched the part of her arm where needle tracks had broken the skin.

"Lewis?"

"No." She shook her head, avoiding eye contact. "This time, I'm talking about my father. Andrew. He was a very horrible person. He got what was coming to him. He used to beat my mother and me. Constantly. Every second night, he would drink too much, and he would beat her first, and when I was old enough to try and stop him, he would beat me second. I went to school so many times with bruises and black eyes, but nobody said anything. Why would nobody say anything? Why wouldn't somebody help me?"

"I don't know, Michelle."

"He tried to hide it. He tried to cover it up. I bet he never told anyone how bad he really was. Under all that public goodwill, he was a despicable man at home."

"He told me." Harvey stepped closer to Michelle, wary of her instability. "He regretted what he did to you and your mother more than anything. It ate him up inside. He worked so hard to make up for those mistakes."

"Mistakes? It was more than that. It was more than just a mistake. His behavior ruined my life. Ruined it. That's more than just a mistake. That's the behavior of an evil man."

"He knew he did wrong. He talked to me about it, Michelle. He was so sorry for what he did. He regretted it every day of his life. He hated himself for doing that to you, and all he wanted in those final years was for you to be happy."

The emotions of the beaten teenage girl, the emotions that she had never let go of, came flooding back, filling her with rage, hatred, and fear. She didn't have the energy to fight it anymore; she didn't have the power to be strong and hold it back. The tears welled up in her eyes as she gripped the railing.

For so long, she had avoided the emotions. She'd tried to mask them with constant hits of heroin, but all that did was sink her further into a pit of self-loathing.

"I never forgave him." She sighed, shaking her head and sniffing away the tears. "Never. I never wanted to forgive him, either. That hatred was a part of me. I couldn't let that go; it was a part of my identity. Instead of hating myself, I could hate him. I could use all that energy to hate him. He was still evil in my eyes."

She scratched the other arm, desperate to avoid looking Harvey in the eye.

"People can redeem themselves, Michelle. Your father spent the last ten years of his life trying to redeem himself. He tried to help so many people, me included, so he could leave a better mark on this world. He wanted to leave this world a good man, not an evil one."

"No matter how much good he did in this world, he damaged my life beyond repair. I have spent my entire adult life addicted to one thing or another, trying to escape the pain of a father who didn't love me. He didn't love me. Why couldn't he love me?" Harvey didn't answer. "I tried to forget it, but I couldn't. It destroyed me. He used to beat me all the time. How could someone do that?"

He didn't answer her question. Instead, he moved

closer, wary of her nervousness. "Why did you call me out here, Michelle?"

"I needed a lawyer. Isn't that what you do?"

"Yes, but what for?"

Michelle started to unroll the piece of paper in her hand. "It's my will. I need a lawyer to sign it, and I knew that my father was close to you. I figured you would help me because you knew my father. That's why I needed you to come here."

"Why here? Why not my office?"

"This is the last place Mom walked before she went into the hospital. She never left the hospital after that. This was the last place she walked free before she died of cancer." She wiped another tear away. "She loved bridges. She loved this place. She loved the breeze in her hair and the sun on her shoulders. She felt free here. This was her place of peace. Her place to escape him." She drew a long breath. "She was the only person to ever love me."

"Your father loved you," Harvey added. "He loved you more than anything."

"He did?" Her voice was desperate. "But he was horrible to me. How could you beat someone that you love?"

Harvey couldn't answer that question. He didn't understand it either. "He regretted his past so much, Michelle. He hated what he did to you and your mother. He used to talk to me about you. He would bring out photos of you, and there was love in his eyes, a smile on his face. His favorite photo was you dressed up as a lion for your elementary school play. You looked so cute."

"He still had that photo?"

"Next to his bed."

That brought a smile to Michelle's face. "I remember that day. I was so nervous before the play, and Dad gave me a great big hug and said everything would be fine. That was one of the only times I really felt his love."

"All he wanted was your forgiveness and your health. He wanted you to be happy."

"I know that… now." She paused again, looking out to the flow of water in front of them. "I finally realize that. The court case made me realize that. All this time, I hated him, and he loved me. And now…" She went to say the words that she had never been able to say. The words caught in her throat.

Harvey waited, providing her with all the time she needed.

"I… I forgive him."

A strong ray of sunshine poked through the gray clouds, a sign from the heavens above.

"I forgive him." A lone tear slowly rolled down her cheek. "It seems so strange to say that. After all those years of hate, after all that anger, I forgive him. That forgiveness only came to me today. I finally picked up the paper and read his obituary. I had it with me for months, but I couldn't bring myself to read it. Today, I read about all the good he had done in the world. All the lives he had changed. All the people he had helped. And I realized that I'm just being one selfish little girl. It's time for me to forgive him. I have been holding onto that hate for so long, and now I almost feel free."

"Almost?"

She rubbed her arm and looked away again. "Almost. There are other things that have trapped me these days."

"Heroin?"

She nodded, ashamed. "But this, this hatred, it consumed me. And… now, finally, it's gone. It's gone."

"Forgiveness can set you free."

"Do you know what it's like to be hurt by someone that you love so much?"

"I do."

"And did you forgive them?"

"I did." He looked to the water, leaning on the handrail. "My brother, Jonathon, became addicted to drugs in his late teens. Heroin. It tore our family apart. He stole from us, abused us, and even hit my dear old mother. Gave her a black eye. After that, I beat him to the ground and told him to leave the house and never return. He left. That was twenty years ago, and I haven't seen him since."

"Do you think he's still addicted to drugs?"

"I hope not. I forgave him for everything that he did a long, long time ago. I only want the best for him now."

Michelle looked at Harvey and whispered, "I just wanted him to love me. I wanted…" She shook her head. "It doesn't matter now."

"What's in the will, Michelle?" As always, Harvey stopped the emotive conversation from digging too far into past hurts.

Michelle looked at the paper in her hands. "After my father's death, I inherited ten million dollars. That was what the old man left me. Ten million dollars. I guess it was his way of saying sorry. I downloaded this standard will form from a website and filled in the blanks. It says I need a lawyer to witness it, so that's why I need you to sign it. I need to make sure that the money goes to the right place after I die."

She shoved the piece of paper into Harvey's hands.

Carefully, in the gently blowing breeze, he opened the piece of paper and read it.

"You're donating the money to The East Rehabilitation Center? The one that Carlos works at? And to the other drug rehab center down the road?"

"That's right. Five million dollars each."

"No one else?"

"No. It's my time for redemption." She scratched her arm again. "It's my time to let go of the past and make sure that money goes where it's needed."

He stared at her, hard and cold.

"Was it the money that made you pull the trigger?"

Her head turned suddenly towards him, surprised by the question. "Sign the paper." She gestured towards the will. "And then I'll answer any questions you have."

He read every word on the page carefully, adding his signature where required, holding the paper on his lap as he signed.

"I need you to sign here." He left an 'x' on the page.

Quickly, she scribbled her name on the page and handed the paper back to him. "I want you to keep it on file for when my time comes."

He nodded and folded the piece of paper in half.

"Was it the money, Michelle? Is that why you shot your father?"

"No." She shook her head, brushing her hair back from her face. "For Juan, it was about the money. He knew that I would have gotten a lot of money from my father's death. He knew how much that old man was worth."

"Then why did you shoot him?"

"Revenge. Freedom. A chance to leave an old life behind." She looked back to the water flowing gently under the bridge. The sun glistened off the little waves in the water, creating a sense of peace in her. "When I looked him in the eyes and pulled the trigger, I thought that I would have felt some sort of satisfaction. I had dreamt about it for years. So many years. Freedom from my abuser. I wanted so much to shoot him. Every time Juan made me go to his house and meet him, I just wanted to shoot him. I imagined that over and over. I wanted to watch him suffer so badly."

"But?"

"But I felt nothing. I didn't feel anything. It wasn't the freedom that I craved. It was nothing. He didn't argue; he didn't even fight back. I had the gun to his head, and he just sat there, almost a smile on his face, and he said that he loved me. That's when I shot him. I expected that moment would bring me freedom, but I felt nothing."

"Where are you going to find that freedom, Michelle?"

"At the end of that road." She nodded to the other side of the bridge, but her reference confused Harvey. "Hold onto that will, Bill Harvey. Drug addicts like me don't generally live that long."

"If you find freedom, you may surprise yourself and live for a very long time."

"I know where my freedom is." She began to walk away from Harvey across the bridge. Despite the lack of pedestrian access, she walked along the side, out of the way of the cars.

Harvey watched her for a while, her steps small, her head held high, and her shoulders back. From this angle, he would never guess she was a drug addict.

Her walk looked free.

Loose.

Happy, almost.

But as she walked across the bridge, she stopped halfway. Awkwardly, she climbed upwards, up the tall metal structure.

The reality of the situation became clear.

"Michelle! No!"

Frantically, he ran towards her.

By the time he made it to her, she was halfway up the towering bridge, too far for him to reach.

"Michelle! No! Michelle!"

"This is my freedom," she called back down to him. "This is my chance to be free from all the pain. This is what I have wanted for so long. I want to be free."

"No, Michelle! There is another way! Let me help you. Please! Come down!"

She smiled as she looked down at him. "You can't help me but hold onto that will. It will help so many people. That's my redemption."

"No!"

Slowly, Michelle Hardgrave stepped her right foot forward…

With the sorrow of a girl who would never escape her addiction, she fell toward the water.

Arms wide, hair flowing, smile on her face.

Finally, she was free.

CHAPTER 31

Feet on his large table, whiskey in one hand and a cigar in the other, Bill Harvey leaned back in his office chair, unsure if he was happy with the outcome of his latest case.

"Could you be any more of a stereotype?" Kate laughed as she stood in the doorway to his office.

"Just enjoying life's finer things, Kate." He took a puff of his cigar. "We're very lucky people. Despite everything that life has thrown at us, our lives are very good. We live happy, meaningful lives that help make a difference in the world."

"Cigars always make you philosophical." Kate grinned again, her slight figure leaning on the doorframe. With her arms folded, and her hair flowing free, she looked like a picture of good health and good will.

"Kate—"

"Can I ask you something, Bill?" She stepped into the room and quietly shut the door behind her.

"Go on." He drew another puff of his cigar. "But remember you're talking to 'Philosophical Bill.'"

"Of course." She smiled and sat down. "Did Michelle Hardgrave kill her father? After her death, Juan Lewis claimed that it wasn't him who pulled the trigger. He's blaming Michelle for pulling the trigger.

Is he just trying to get off the charges, or is there truth in what he's saying?"

"Who knows?" Harvey lied. "But if Michelle did kill her father, then she wouldn't have been entitled to the inheritance. It would be the fortitude ruling, and because she received the inheritance as a result of her crime, she wouldn't have received a cent. Her will would be invalid."

"Where would the money have gone then?"

"Back to the estate. Then who knows where the money would have gone? There would have been legal battles for years over that money. But this way, with Juan Lewis, charged with Judge Hardgrave's death; her inheritance goes to people it can help. I don't think anyone is going to argue over that."

"So just because the money has gone to good use, we should just forget about it?"

"Juan Lewis is a criminal. No doubt about it. He has been his whole life, and he was in the room when Judge Hardgrave died. It doesn't matter now who pulled the trigger. Lewis deserves his time behind bars. And Lewis has already sold Miles out, which means both Lewis and Miles are behind bars right now. That's a win in my books."

The sound of the front office door opening caught their attention.

"Carlos is here." Kate stood and began to exit his office.

"Send him in." Harvey smiled genuinely. "And Kate?"

"Yes, Bill?"

Their eyes connected.

His heart skipped a beat.

Her breath caught in her throat.

"I—"

"My favorite people!" Carlos interrupted their moment.

Harvey broke eye contact with his secretary. "Hello, Carlos."

Walking into the office with the confidence of a man who had faced prison and walked away, Carlos López had a spring in his step that Harvey hadn't seen before.

Harvey looked back to the door, but the slim figure of Kate Spencer had already disappeared.

"So what happens now?" Carlos smiled as he talked.

"You walk away a free man and live out the rest of your life."

"Just like that?"

"Just like that."

"Wow. I didn't think this was actually going to be the outcome. As we were going through that trial, I thought that I was definitely going to have to jump back over the border and go back to Mexico and live my life. I thought there was no doubt about it. I was done for sure. But somehow, you turned it around. The star hypnotherapist turned lawyer. You worked your magic, Mr. Harvey."

"No magic involved." Harvey threw his hands up in the air. "Just a bit of luck."

"It was more than luck."

"I couldn't have guessed that he was going to take the blame for the drugs. I didn't see that coming, especially after he sold you out on the stand."

Once Juan Lewis realized he was going to spend the rest of his life behind bars charged with the murder of Judge Hardgrave, he took the blame for the briefcase full of drugs.

It was his way of taking the fall for his cousin.

"He didn't want to sell me out," Carlos stated. "They forced him to. The prosecution made him sell out Miles and blame the drug charges on me, or they would have thrown him in prison. He told me that they raided another house of his and found another briefcase. He struck a deal to escape those charges, but he didn't expect to be taking on the blame for the murder."

"You're lucky that he did take the blame for the drugs."

Carlos smiled. "My family."

"He didn't sound much like family when he tried to blame you while he was on the stand."

"We all make mistakes. And most people make an effort to correct them. He made a mistake, and then he made the effort to correct it. I forgive him for that." Carlos shrugged. "And in my line of work, most of the people that walk through our doors have made mistakes. They're all drug users who have seen the worst life has to offer. You have to be able to forgive the people who make an effort to do better in life."

"You're a good man, Carlos."

"I try." Carlos shrugged. "Are you worried about Lewis and Miles coming after you?"

"The problem with guys like Lewis and Miles is that their 'friends' always disappear quickly when they're thrown in prison. Nobody wants to be associated with a criminal—especially not one that's convicted of murdering a judge. I wouldn't be worried about Lewis' high-powered friends. They're as fickle as they come. They'll have forgotten about him already. But his people on the street, they're another thing."

Carlos laughed. "Don't be worried about those guys. Someone else has already stepped up to take Lewis' spot. Someone else is already covering the operations. He's already a forgotten man on the street, too. Nobody on the street cares about him anymore."

"That's good to hear." Harvey took a sip of his whiskey.

"So that's it? Are we all done?"

"Not quite. You've been charged with contempt of court for lying about your whereabouts on the day of the raid, but due to your good work in the community, they're only giving you a small fine. That notice will come in the mail, and I suggest that you pay the fine and forget about it. And considering you almost helped a man get away with murder, I think you've gotten off very lucky."

"I'm sorry, Bill. If I had known what he was going to do that day, I would never have agreed to cover for him and be his false alibi. I had no idea that he was going to shoot the judge. I wouldn't have let him go if I knew. He must have been angry that Michelle didn't want anything to do with him anymore. And if Michelle got off the drugs, Lewis had no power over the judge. I guess all the power just got to his head. He thought he was untouchable."

"The killer is no longer on the streets now. That's what matters. Judge Hardgrave can now rest in peace. His daughter forgave him in the end, and in her will, she asked to be buried next to him."

"And the money that she donated will go a long way. The rehab center survived on very little for so long, but even with the money, we'll keep the same philosophy at the center. We'll make sure that her donation will make a difference in people's lives."

"That's wonderful, Carlos. It truly is."

Carlos reached into his jacket pocket. "I don't have a lot of possessions, but as a symbol of my gratitude, I want to give you this photo of the people that you've helped. These are the people that have just graduated from our drug rehabilitation process. You've helped these people, Bill. This is my way of saying thanks from the people that you've saved. These are the people who get another chance because you kept me out of prison. This wasn't about me. The win was for them."

Harvey took the photo from Carlos' hands.

"Look at those people, Bill. Look at them. Those are the men and women that you've helped. Those are the lives that you've rescued." Carlos stood up. "Those are the people that are really thanking you."

"Wait."

"What is it?"

Harvey drew a long, deep breath. "All these people in this photo—they're all recovered drug addicts?"

"That's right. These are the people who graduated in the last group, the recovery group. All of these people have been clean for at least one year."

Harvey stared at the picture, long and hard, his head spinning.

"What is it, Bill?" Carlos leaned forward as Harvey stared at the picture.

"That man in the top left corner."

"Yes? Do you know him?"

A smile drifted across Harvey's face. "Yes, Carlos, I do."

"An old friend?"

"That man is more than a friend." Bill Harvey's eyes filled with tears. "Carlos, that man is my brother."

THE END

ALSO BY PETER O'MAHONEY

In the Bill Harvey Series:

FIRE AND JUSTICE
WILL OF JUSTICE
A TIME FOR JUSTICE
TRUTH AND JUSTICE

In the Joe Hennessy Legal Thriller Series:

THE SOUTHERN LAWYER
THE SOUTHERN CRIMINAL
THE SOUTHERN KILLER
THE SOUTHERN TRIAL

In the Jack Valentine Series:

GATES OF POWER
THE HOSTAGE
THE SHOOTER
THE THIEF
THE WITNESS

In the Tex Hunter Legal Thriller series:

POWER AND JUSTICE
FAITH AND JUSTICE
CORRUPT JUSTICE
DEADLY JUSTICE
SAVING JUSTICE
NATURAL JUSTICE
FREEDOM AND JUSTICE
LOSING JUSTICE
FAILING JUSTICE
FINAL JUSTICE

Printed in Dunstable, United Kingdom